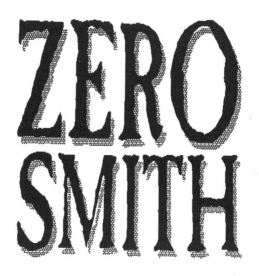

# ZERO SMITH

## A Western by K. Imus

KEICO COMPANY
407 NW 132nd Street
Seattle, WA 98177

International Standard Book No. 0-9653584-0-2
Library of Congress Card No. 96-94725

Imus, K.
*Zero Smith*

Printed in United States of America

To obtain copies of *Zero Smith* by K. Imus, contact
your local  bookstore, library, or write to the Keico
Company.

*Published*
*by*

**KEICO COMPANY**
**407 NW 132nd Street**
**Seattle, WA  98177**
**Fax: 206-361-6249**

*To Nancy 3/27/97*
*a New Sun Valley lady*

## ACKNOWLEDGMENTS

*[signature]*

To Hal Imus, Doc Roberts and Alvin Teag of the Crooked H Ranch, Camp Verde, Arizona

To C. B. and Jack Rich of the Double Arrow Ranch, Seeley Lake, Montana

To Gordon Sims, first mate on the brig, Lady Washington, Bainbridge Island, Washington

For their patience with me

and

To the women I have known.

# ZERO
# SMITH

# LEARN TO LISTEN
# TO THE RAVEN, THE CROW
# AND ONE'S OWN MUSE


## K. IMUS

# CHAPTER ONE

Zero Smith was a man with no beginning, no past, a dubious present and certainly no future. One day he just appeared. He was a marked man, a gunfighter. The best. Many said, "The best ever."

Zero Smith knew better. There was one man who was his equal or perhaps even better. The man who taught him. His friend Jonathan Galway.

Since the latter part of the Civil War, Smith had been all hollow inside. He felt nothing, not even for his horse. Smith's highly developed survival instincts functioned very well, but the rest of Zero Smith was entirely shut off.

His life in the West was as much of a surprise to Smith as it was to his family and associates. Before the war he had fully intended to take his place in running the family enterprises, but the war changed all of that, and all he wanted to do was disappear into open country and not see anyone, which he did.

# Zero Smith

He had simply wired his family "not coming home now" and ridden west.

Many men came back from the war with no visible wounds on the outside but with dreadful wounds to the mind. Smith was one of these men, but he didn't seem to know or care. He was dour and sometimes mean yet wasn't aware of it.

He was a marked man. Every gun slick and would-be hotshot who was out to make a gunman's reputation, wanted to try him. Several had tried and so far, all had failed. He wasn't even scratched. Those men that lived had a shot up gun hand and their career as a gunslinger was over. Worse yet, they felt naked. Each man felt very vulnerable and exposed—and they were.

No one believed that a man in a gunfight would actually shoot just the gun hand of his opponent. Yet that is just what Zero Smith did. He didn't believe in killing unless it was necessary. It had been necessary a few times because those men were fast, very fast.

When in a gunfight, Zero Smith did not read the eyes of his adversary. He read movement. Hand movement. He had a kind of vision that focused minutely on any movement, even peripheral movement. Once he had actually shot up a cat as it ran into his side vision during a gun battle. When they found the cat, even Zero was surprised. The frightened cat had nearly got Zero killed because there was a man trying to shoot Smith just as the cat jumped into the line of fire. Zero had to fire a second time, this one at the moving man who was trying to kill him. Only Smith's incredible gun speed saved his life. Smith's peripheral vision was correct, but it was unfortunate that the furry little critter had clouded it for a split second and got himself sent to cat heaven.

Usually in a showdown, Smith watched the man's gun hand. When the hand moved he willed a .44 bullet into it. He had the kind of shooting accuracy that few believed even when they saw it. Many people had said, "No one is that fast." Yet there it was.

The ultimate insult to a gunman was to shoot up his gun hand. This would end his career, destroy his ego and put him out of business for good. When word got out, it would frequently bring out the man's enemies as well. Zero Smith did this on purpose.

Smith's father, away on a business trip, had been accidentally killed by a hotshot gunslinger's stray bullet. Smith was fifteen years old. The boy felt the loss deeply. He and his father were very close, but there was a rift between them at the time that had never been repaired.

# Zero Smith

The loss of his father stayed with Smith in an unhealthy way. At showdown time he was really shooting the man who killed his father. He had another edge that even he was not aware of, and that was he simply didn't care if he lived or not. The war had tapped him out. He was like a sleep walker who was dried up inside. He was as dry as an old harness.

It was early morning and Smith was riding across some high meadow country that was heavily frosted. There were vast beautiful panoramic views in all directions. The countryside was laced with little ice cold streams that had come alive with the end of winter. In the draws were willow and aspen groves by now turned to a full green. The sun, just after dawn, was a huge deep red ball, momentarily perched on the very edge of a far off mountain. Soon it would burn off the cold damp fog in the low places and put the frost away until the next time.

Zero Smith noticed none of this. He was barely aware that he was cold. The sun was a welcome sight to his horse and the town up ahead was an ugly sight to Zero Smith. It wasn't much of a place, but he needed ammunition and had come for that purpose.

Smith read a sign that said, "Eats", and pulled up. He tied his horse and went in. The place was warm inside and several of the locals were already around the big pot bellied stove trying to get the chill out of their bones.

When Smith entered, they all looked up and the place got quiet as though none of them had ever seen a stranger before.

Smith was used to that look. It was fear. The people could feel it. There was a cold hard look in the eyes of Zero Smith. He sat with his back to the wall and ordered breakfast.

When he'd finished eating he walked two doors up the street to the general store, bought his ammo and returned to the restaurant for a second cup of coffee.

In that short time he'd been spotted and challenged to a gunfight. Smith acted like he didn't think the young man was talking to him and proceeded to enter the restaurant.

Now here he was about to face another hick town tinhorn. The local fast gun. The young man had heard of the legendary fast gun and only suspected that the stranger in town was not just any old Smith, but in fact the notorious Zero Smith. There was a sinister something about the way Smith wore his gun. Zero gave the man credit for having a sharp eye. He'd picked Smith out from dozens of other hard looking men that were around town.

The young man came strutting into the

# Zero Smith

grubby restaurant in front of half of the dried up town. Perhaps they were desperate for entertainment. Zero was seated at a table finishing his coffee when the man challenged him a second time. Smith didn't even look up.

The local fast gun paraded his contempt for Smith. He strutted and sneered. He talked to the patrons in the restaurant and casually pointed at Smith with great disdain. The challenge called for a quick draw at noon the next day on Front Street.

Smith let the man go on and on. He had never seen anyone so full of himself. When he had finished his coffee, he stood up, walked over to the young man, slapped the man's face three times, very hard, and took his gun away. Then he walked out of the restaurant carrying the man's gun. Smith hadn't said a word. The patrons were stunned and the fast gun had tears in his eyes, both from pain and humiliation.

This local fast gun had intimidated the entire town and Zero Smith had treated him like a child and showed the town what the young man really was in seconds, a loud mouth bully.

It was all too dramatic. Smith thought to himself that he would just stay long enough to teach the fellow a lesson and perhaps save his life, but he didn't care enough to do even that. His second thought was to ride on out, and he did. In fact, he rode on for over a hundred miles. To the locals a hundred miles was half way around the world. He figured and rightly, that he was safe from the hot dog gunman back there. It was a nuisance, but he had moved before and it was better than killing a man, or in this case a boy-man.

Smith wanted total obscurity. No fame, no accolades and certainly no fear from his fellow man. Mostly he wanted to be left alone, to hide from his gun reputation. This he did, very successfully.

Zero Smith was elusive. He had a knack of not being noticed, even in a crowd of one. He dressed like a hayseed, shuffled like a hayseed and even chewed on straw occasionally if it helped to confuse the sheriff and send the poor man "that-a-way."

Smith reasoned that if he went around shooting holes in people, sooner or later he would have to deal with the law. His gunfights were always fair fights, if there is such a thing. The code of the west said there was, and as there were usually witnesses, there was little trouble with the law.

The chameleon role worked well for him, too. Zero Smith could almost blend in with the woodwork when necessary. If he stayed in a town after a gunfight, he slipped into

# Zero Smith

the hayseed role. The investigating sheriff was always convinced that anyone that slow in the brain pan couldn't possibly be a fast gun, so it was assumed Smith had just made a lucky shot.

Smith was always well-mounted but the horse he was riding these days was very special. The critter was a beautiful big sorrel stud with four white socks, a white blaze and a yellow mane and tail. He was well-gaited, fast, came to a whistle, and was a good watch dog. For some reason the horse was fond of Smith though he received little affection in return. Smith had won the horse in a card game.

The horse had belonged to a wealthy fool. Smith played a better than average game of poker because he was smart and he had money to back his cards. He knew what had appeared on the table, and he guessed he had the man beat with his full house against the fellow's two pair.

They kept calling and raising until the local was out of money, so he bet his horse. The man was used to buying a hand now and then because he typically carried more money than most men. He thought he was going to buy this one as well because Smith was dressed like most saddle tramps. He had warn down heels on warn out boots, a coat with a big hole in the elbow caused by a careless, and now dead, knife fighter. His hat was old several years back. Only his guns were in first class shape, but even they were different. They featured hair triggers and removed front sights. Smith owned several six guns, but he only wore one at a time. One was usually enough.

Zero accepted the horse as a bet sight unseen. People said it was a great horse. To everyone's surprise, Smith put up enough cash against the horse to make it fair to all those present, and called.

Zero Smith won the hand, he won the horse and he killed the fool that drew on him in front of about twenty witnesses. He talked to the sheriff who had heard of him and Smith agreed to move on. He was sure the horse was worth it the first time he rode him. The horse was smooth as silk.

Lazing along on a bright spring day, Zero Smith wasn't aware of the beauty around him. He stopped by a small stream and pulled the saddle from his horse. He was going to eat and have a nap. The nap was something he did from time to time. He ate a quick snack while sitting on his bed roll and promptly fell asleep. The horse was doing guard duty.

These two had been riding together long enough to have faith in one another. The faithful horse was an excellent watch dog and

# Zero Smith

the faithless owner would probably have shot the nag, if he failed to sound an alarm if there were any real danger.

Zero Smith was a little light on compassion these days. There were several gun wizards that could attest to that fact. He was still beat up from the war but didn't know it. Smith was unaware that he walked with a heavier step than most men. He rode roughshod over nearly everything.

One time in a small cow town bar down on the Canadian River, Zero was challenged by the local fast gun. The man noticed that Smith was a stranger in town and began to ask questions in a very rude way. Smith loved to take on these loud mouths.

"Hey you, I'm talking to you, saddle bum," said the local loud mouth.

Smith disarmed the man by shooting one bullet that trashed the man's gun hand for life, and blew the useless pistol right out of the holster. Then he shot the man in the knee. Smith looked around the bar and said, "Anyone else?"

No one spoke. They didn't even breathe. They were stunned. It all happened so fast.

Smith finished his drink and walked out. No one followed him. Apparently, none of their Mamma's had raised any foolish children.

On another occasion when Zero Smith

was near Santa Fe, he had just finished a meal when he watched an American cattleman slap a Mexican woman. Smith was seated across the room and when the man attempted to slap the woman a second time, Smith shot him through both hands. No one realized what had happened except Smith, who holstered his gun and continued to finish his coffee as though the quarrel between the cattleman and the woman had been none of his business. And it wasn't, so long as the big, mean and ugly, two hundred pound man didn't try to slap the petite and lovely, hundred and five pound, pretty Mexican woman.

The cattleman was in a whole lot of hurt and the woman was very pleased to see him suffer and said so. She walked over to Smith's table and sat down to thank him. The woman explained the situation which Smith could have cared less about, but he tried to listen attentively. Finally the woman suggested that Zero Smith should be careful because the man he had shot was very powerful in these parts and would undoubtedly make trouble for him.

Smith said to her, "May I borrow a few horses from you to cover my trail?"

"Si, amigo, anything you want. We have several in the corral. When you turn them loose, they will come home."

"Thank you, miss."

# Zero Smith

Zero went out back and with the help of a young boy the lady had sent to help, gathered the horses and rode west. The horses herded at a run easily with two wranglers. Shortly after leaving town, Smith headed them into the timber. After several miles he had the boy chase three horses in one direction and drop off a horse every mile, and he did the same in another direction until he was down to three horses. He herded these last three horses to some large rock outcropping and then sent the mob up and across the solid rock surfaces for as far as he could. Finally, he scattered them all in different directions. He doubted if the average tracker could follow his tracks. Zero knew full well that a track, made by a horse carrying a rider is very different from a riderless horse track, but he hoped riding over the rock would be enough to confuse anyone who might have been able to follow him this far. It was.

Smith learned by traveling alone and by staying away from people were the best ways for him to avoid trouble. He'd been doing just that for some time—perhaps for two years—and things were getting better when he stopped to think about it. He'd been in fewer brawls and fewer gunfights. He had destroyed less property and from his point of view he might almost begin to call himself a model citizen. There were a couple of exceptions. For example, he recalled an incident a few weeks back where a group of the village bad guys wanted to tar and feather him because he shot up one of their friends in a saloon gunfight.

Smith had only shot the fellow in his gun hand, and the locals thought it to be just a lucky shot. They were sure that he was really trying to kill the fellow. The wounded man was known as the fastest gun in the area, so his pals were sure the traveling through saddle tramp had just been lucky.

Smith, who watched his back trail as well as his front trail, saw them clouding dust and waited in an opportune spot for four of the village idiots to arrive. When they did, he set off a bomb of dynamite sticks that he sometimes carried, with a hand gun, that sounded as though it would blow up their half of the world. There was no lead in it but there sure was a lot of noise. The bomb scared their horses, which promptly went to bucking and toppled two of the riders. The concussion deafened all four men and probably the horses for a time. Then he roped the two men who were still astride and hoisted them up, arms pinned to their sides, to hang from a tree limb upside down. They had a few rope burns but they would live. It cost Zero a good rope but he replaced it with one of the other fellow's ropes. Then Smith took the guns from

## Zero Smith

their holsters and shot the boot heels from their boots. He drove their horses five miles ahead of him and then turned them loose.

The men were lucky, but only one man among them thought so. He was probably the only one among them with sense enough to live to old age.

# CHAPTER TWO

Most western towns were pretty much the same. Some were just meaner than others. None had been all that kind to Zero Smith, nor did he expect them to be. He didn't even think about it. He was just too dry inside to notice much of anything except his back trail, which he watched with great care. He did have a keen eye for trouble. It had been honed to a fine edge during the war and even now, years later, his personal war was still going on. To put it bluntly, Zero Smith was a survivor.

He had incredible gun skill, but to keep it he had to spend many hours practicing his quick draw, and shooting seemed to bleed off some of his anger, so he practiced a lot.

His mantra went round and round inside his head "faster, faster, faster," until he was the best. It was a holy mission. His anger drove him to practice. And with each practice session, he was always driven by the mantra chant that said, "faster, faster."

He wore an aura of menace around him-

# Zero Smith

self, the way other men wore clothes. When people looked into his eyes they were afraid and moved away. Most of the men Smith killed had friends and each one became his enemy. He was so angry sometimes he even looked forward to meeting these so-called enemies.

To the men who had faced him in a gunfight, Smith became the Devil incarnate. They saw it in his eyes just before they died. Smith was aware of this quality that he had and used it occasionally so as to be left alone. Would-be gunmen had backed down just from looking him in the eye. He had changed. He had become nearly evil.

Zero Smith was actually very wealthy. His family was made up of eastern Yankee business people and he had inherited a fortune before the war that was more than doubled by his managers during the war. His soul had been pauperized by the war but not his pocketbook.

He stuffed wool into his ears and practiced with his pistols for long hours every day. It helped to dispel some of his always present anger. He went through many guns and a small fortune in ammunition. The gun practice calloused his hands and put strength in his wrists. He worked on speed. His old mantra was always there like a second person, the voice of his teacher, Jonathan Galway, whispering, then talking, then shouting, then even screaming in his mind, "faster, faster, faster." The voice was insatiable. It always wanted more speed, more speed. He had tripled his speed and the voice still wanted more. "Draw and shoot" became his chant, his code, his only challenge in life. He could always shoot very accurately, but during these years he concentrated on speed.

He filed the triggers, he sanded the grips, he removed the front sight on all of his pistols. He finally settled on a .44 caliber Remington top-strap with a shortened barrel. He had this gun tailored by a smith who removed a half inch of the gun barrel and filed the firing mechanism to a hair trigger. It would have been a fast weapon in any shooter's hand, but in the hand of Zero Smith it was pure lightning.

He rarely went to towns except to replace his practice weapons and buy a few supplies. Other than that he lived out under the stars. It was a long time before he could sleep through the night without jumping up several times, gun in hand. It was even longer before he sought the company of others, a woman occasionally, and even then, as with the merchants, he was nearly nonverbal. A silent man who moved from place to place like a shadow. He never smiled nor answered questions in an area that was known for hav-

## Zero Smith

ing few askers. Local sheriffs would frequently ask if he was staying long. They were always uncomfortable when he just looked at them and didn't reply.

# CHAPTER THREE

Usually when Smith needed supplies or he felt it was necessary to deal with bankers or sheriffs, lawyers or merchants, he adopted the role of a dull-witted, hayseed cowhand. He got into that mode before arriving at this next town.

Changing roles for Smith was easy. He simply did what amounted to changing a few clothes and his personality. He put on baggy, bib overalls, a sloppy old hat and funny farmer shoes and he usually chewed on a straw. He spoke using a southern, "back in the hills" accent that was really not from anywhere. Except for the gun belt, he seemed to be a completely different person.

Four days later he arrived in a different town. This one had some shade trees and some painted buildings. There were planted flowers in boxes on the main drag. It seemed a pleasant enough place, and there was a small stream that meandered through the town.

Smith entered the town by riding over a

# Zero Smith

bridge to the main street. There was a sign on the bridge that claimed this was the town of Pinedale.

There were the usual stores, restaurants, shops and stables but unlike most western towns, the main street was dotted with huge shade trees such as maple, cottonwood, willow, pine and aspen.

He pulled up in front of a weather worn, false fronted, freight office and read a sign that said, "Teamster Wanted."

He climbed down, walked up to the porch, tore the sign off the wall and went in the door marked "Office."

The inside of the building smelled musty and was as colorless and warn as the outside. The place needed paint. There were dusty files beside a well worn counter. A tired overhead fan limped around in boring circles trying not to disturb the musty air. Dead flies were suspended in webs in the window corners and a huge calico cat opened one eye at the disturbance created when Zero moved toward the counter.

He was met by a very attractive lady who looked as though she didn't belong there .

Smith said, "Mam."

"You tore my sign down," she said.

"Mam."

He noticed she had wonderful sky blue-grey eyes that peeked out from behind long lashes. Her eyes, at the moment, were full of fire. She was perturbed and mumbled something about another slow paying customer. She also had long, beautiful, honey colored hair. It was swept back from her face and held with a large comb on each side. The rest fell down behind her head to the middle of her back—all except for one long, aggravating, S-shaped curl, which she blew out of her eyes every few seconds. Her face wore high cheek bones and a good, broad forehead. Below those magnificent eyes was a small straight nose, under which resided a generously full-lipped, wide mouth that puckered when she talked.

The front of her blouse looked like everything on the inside wanted out, and her skirt was wrapped sensuously around her long, long legs. Smith thought her a goddess, and as he was to learn, so did most men in the town of Pinedale.

Zero Smith was having a very difficult time staying in the dull-witted role which required staring at the floor, when what he really wanted to do was look right at her and devour this curvaceous visual feast.

When Smith was in his posture that shouted humble, hayseed loser, to most folks, he would simply slouch, shuffle when he walked, chew a straw, and talk in a perfect southern hayseed, back-in-the hills drawl.

# Zero Smith

When questioned about anything having to do with his past, he simply would stare at the floor and say, "Must have been some other Smith." They were always convinced. The questioners figured that nobody this dull could possibly be the fast gun wizard they had heard so much about.

He could slip in and out of his character role at the blink of an eye. He was so good at it that when he changed back to the real Smith, people would swear that he was a different person.

Smith was in the hayseed character role at the moment and intended to stay that way while in this town. It helped to avoid trouble.

"You tore my sign down."

Smith was mute.

Again the pretty lady repeated herself.

"You tore my sign down."

"Yes, mam."

He looked forlorn and handed her the sign. The pretty lady who was flustered before he appeared, was now becoming very exasperated.

Smith, keeping a straight face, just stood there and stared at the floor.

"Well, are you a teamster, or do you just go around tearing down people's signs?"

"Yes, mam. I mean, no, mam. Oh, I'm a teamster all right. Yes, mam."

"And stop calling me mam."

"Yes, mam."

"Oh, go on out to the back. Old John will show you where to start."

Miss Laura didn't mention money and Smith didn't ask. Smiling on the inside but outwardly just as poker faced as before, Smith shuffled out to find that Old John had been listening. He was smiling, too.

Old John, Zero was to learn, was a sly old fox. He had been born a slave and been bought and freed by Miss Laura's father, Mr. Samuel Karen, when Laura was four years old. He'd been a friend and confidant and employed ever since by the Karen Freight Company.

Mr. Sam had died suddenly seven months ago, from heart failure, and since then Miss Laura had been running the outfit by herself. Smith thought it a tough business for such a young lass. He surmised that along with being beautiful she must have spunk and brains.

He looked over the stock and the worn harnesses, the tired wagons and guessed closely as to the financial condition of the company. She might slow pay him but he didn't care, for Zero Smith had money. Lots of money.

His first move was to repair a wagon wheel. He figured as to how he was the only driver, he sure didn't want the wheels to fall

# Zero Smith

off while he was out on the road. Next he selected the best pieces of harness equipment so as to have one reasonably good outfit for the team of horses.

He consulted Old John about the stock and settled on a bay and a black with a bald face. The horses were both geldings and to Smith's surprise, they were named Brig and Bark after types of sailing ships.

Samuel Karen, the founder of the company, had been a seafaring man in his youth. He said that by naming the stock after ships it would help remind him of the rough life of the square riggers, a life he was glad to be away from.

The sailor's life was not for everyone. Sam Karen signed on a whaler that took him from Boston around the Horn to the Pacific. The ship provisioned at the port of Lahaina on Maui in the Hawaiian Islands.

Hawaii was great, but the trip around Cape Horn cost Sam Karen considerably. He lost two fingers due to frostbite and a few teeth due to bad food and scurvy.

The return trip was even worse. The ship was loaded and deeper in the water and she wallowed for weeks in mountainous seas as they tried rounding the Horn against the prevailing winds.

The ship tacked back and forth for days and then was blown backwards enough to be right back where she started and have it to do all over again. Sam Karen was a main mast top gallant man. On a brig it was the highest sail, so when the ship rolled in the trough, he and his mate had the wildest ride of any of the crew. It was no place for the faint of heart, particularly during the times of high winds and sleet.

The men lived with ice, dense fog and sleet. Climbing aloft to trim or replacing rotted sails in ice cold, howling winds was enough to make a body wish he were anyplace but the Horn. He made an oath to himself that if he lived through this whaling trip he would drop his anchor someplace warm.

When Sam Karen's daughter asked why he sometimes referred to himself as a "Jacktar", he explained that sailors' hands were often cracked so badly from the wet and cold, that they smeared their hands with tar. The tar left permanent little tattoo-like marks on their hands. Also, the men's clothes always had tar smears from the rigging of the ships.

"Jacktar" was really a British navy expression. The British flag was called the Union Jack. He explained further that the Jack part was the name given to British sailors because they sailed under that flag.

Whaling was a hard life. Except for provisioning in the Hawaiian Islands, the ships

# Zero Smith

stayed at sea in search of whales until their oil casks were filled. Then it was a long, hard, wet return trip of many months to Boston. There were times when most of the crew had boils, lice and many of them also contracted scurvy.

Living in wet clothes and sleeping in wet bunks for weeks at a time, to say nothing of the poor food, was enough to teach Samuel Karen that the sailor's life was not for him. He signed off in Boston after two years on a whaler. He had endured the "Iron men on wooden ships" for two long years and by GOD, that was enough.

Sam Karen drifted to warmer climes intending to plant his feet in the Southwest, and he did. Sometime later he drifted to Pinedale where he met Laura's mother. They married after a brief courtship. Two years later Laura arrived, and they were a happy family until the mother died of pneumonia when Laura was twelve.

Since the death of his wife, Sam Karen was less than a happy man. He did manage to raise and provide for Laura, which most everyone agreed was a task well worth doing, for Laura was an enchantress. The nice kind.

Miss Laura came out to the freight yard with the news that they had a shipment of farm implements to take to the next town, twenty-two miles west of Pinedale. Smith would be gone three or four days. With some strong doubts and anxious misgivings, she gave him the bills of lading, a lunch, and sent him on his way, wondering if she would see him or her wagons ever again.

It was a beautiful morning. The sun had burned off the chill that always lays on the ground at these high altitudes, for Pinedale was tucked snugly into a valley that was about five thousand feet high. Even the horses seemed to be enjoying the walk after resting for a few days.

The country west of Pinedale was mostly flat, centered in a big valley that had many large aspen groves, cottonwoods and willows and large stands of pine, with gentle rolling hills to north and south. He crossed many small streams fed by snow melt from the many high peaks all around. The area was filled with game. Smith saw many antelope and deer, a few elk and a red fox. The sky was home to eagles, hawks and vultures and a hundred kinds of little birds that were all going about the business of living here in the high country.

Some stream crossings were over bridges and some small creeks he had to drive through. There was good grass in the vast meadows and big timber in several areas.

Along every stream there were huge old

# Zero Smith

shade trees where he would occasionally stop to swim or have a nap. He would rest the horses and eat part of the lunch Laura prepared for him. This first trip went well.

When he arrived, he found the town dustier and with less shade than Pinedale, but a nice enough place. Smith thought the townspeople probably had a little less poetry in their soul than the people of Pinedale. The observation marked a subtle beginning of a change in Zero Smith.

Smith had no difficulty on the trip and also had a chance to see some of the beautiful country to the west of Pinedale.

He rented a horse for a few hours and rode the open grass lands to the north. He watched a hawk sail across the sky until it was out of sight. He liked everything he saw. This country pleased him. It was beautiful and good to look at, and it was good country for beef.

He was able to get a return load, which pleased Laura. He made several trips after that and soon became a trusted, if apparently dull-witted, employee.

These trips allowed Smith to see most of the country around Pinedale and he liked it. He started taking his own horse along to have him handy to ride the country. In this way he was able to see much more of the land and still do business for the Karen Freight

Company. He noticed the country was high enough to be green most of the year. There was good grass and wild flowers in the immense meadows. There were two lakes nearby and the stream through Pinedale was head-watered in these lakes. Many-a-time Zero saw great fat trout jumping and suspected that it was a fisherman's paradise.

The lakes were fed by the runoff from the high saw-toothed mountain peaks. The shaded north sides held great stands of pine trees. They also held snow fields until late summer. The lakes, instead of being ice cold, were shallow enough to warm up to swimming comfort by midsummer. They also acted as the main water supply for all of the cattle in the area.

The area was shaded in summer, here and there, by a wide variety of trees. There were evergreens, predominantly pines, some juniper and cedar, cottonwood and vine maple, aspen and willow and enough other vegetation to make fall a great golden spectacle. Smith thought if he hung around here long enough to see the leaves turn, he might learn to believe in God.

It was actually the first time Smith had noticed much of anything in the way of natural beauty since before the war. It had taken Laura, the resident angel, and this near paradise to get his attention. He didn't know it

## Zero Smith

yet, but he was beginning to mend.

# CHAPTER FOUR

Laura breathed a sigh of relief when Old John told her Smith had returned from his latest trip. She was just beginning to trust this hayseed employee when somewhat to her annoyance and surprise, Smith arrived with a payload and a very attractive woman seated on the driver's seat beside him. Judging from the low-cut neckline blouse and very short, split scarlet skirt, which allowed a lot of pretty leg to show above a pretty, black silk garter each time she moved, the woman was obviously a dance hall girl.

Smith and the lady were all smiles and even the horses seemed to be chipper when they should have been worn out.

The scene smacked of hanky-panky, what with the horses being so rested and all, and the big dumb grin on Zero's face.

Candy, for that was her name, looked like the cat that swallowed the canary. It's doubtful if anyone in Pinedale ever looked as pleased as she did at the moment.

Zero hoped, with slim chance, that no

one would notice and almost no one did except for Old John, Laura, the blacksmith across the way, the many store owners and their customers, the livery stable help, and everyone on the main street including a few dogs and cats in the town of Pinedale.

Candy, who was low on brains and long on body, was a provocative beauty. Her head may have been full of fluff, but she was smart enough to know that she had a dynamite figure and that most men were pussycats where she was concerned. She liked being noticed and had proudly waved to the populace from the wagon as she rode into town, as if she were the parade queen of a harvest festival instead of just another new hooker in town.

The men waved back and smiled, and their dreary wives scowled ferociously at Candy, at Smith, at their husbands and at everything that moved. They even scowled at each other as if some unforgivable secret had been found out. Which it had.

One woman was so annoyed with her husband's joyful greeting of Candy that she slapped his face and kicked a dog that was sleeping on the walk. The dog looked up as if to say, "What did I do?

The sheepish husband simply said, "Oops."

Smith was having great fun with all of this on the inside, but outwardly he tried to appear all business. He was trying to appear oblivious to it all, and as dull as usual.

When the team was parked in the yard, he tried to help the leggy Candy down but she had other ideas. She put her arms around Smith's neck and slowly slithered snakelike down the full length of his frame. In the process her skirt climbed up above her pretty little ass to the great joy of the men watching and the great chagrin of the women. Zero Smith almost blushed and grinned big as life. Candy simply giggled.

They were met by Old John, the hostler and all around handy man who was wearing his biggest smile.

Smith said, "Candy, this is John. He does most of the work around here in the yard and all of the thinking and is kind of showing me the ropes."

John beamed.

Candy giggled and shook John's hand.

They went on inside to the office where Smith did the introductions again as he handed Laura some cash.

"Candy, this here's my boss, Miss Laura Karen." He said it as though Laura was way above "us lesser folk" and in many ways she was.

"Miss Karen, this is Candy."

"I'll just bet she is."

This was said with an icy stare. Candy

didn't seem to notice the slight and neither woman cared that Candy's last name was not mentioned.

Candy just giggled.

"Isn't he handsome?" she confided to Laura, as if they were old friends and alone, "but he needs new clothes. As soon as I get to working, I intend to buy him some."

Candy giggled.

Laura resented the girl's possessiveness as she looked at Smith, really for the first time, and realized that he was indeed handsome. Very.

To Laura, Smith said, "The lady was stranded and needed a lift to the next town and that was here so you can see I had to bring her along."

Zero made out as though that explained everything. Then he started to move off with Candy, who was still all giggles and spilling out of the top of her dress. He turned back, and looking at the floor, solemnly explained to Laura in his hayseed drawl, "It was the Christian thing to do."

Laura, who was more then a little steamed by this time, thought to herself that neither of these people had ever been within a mile of a Christian.

However, he did bring back a paying load and a paying customer, and he is off duty. Watching them leave she wondered why she was perturbed.

Old John, who was watching all of this, thought to himself, "That man has style. He goes out with lumber and comes back with a payload and a paying customer who is one very sexy 'lady.'"

Old John thought to himself, "Miss Giggles don't talk much, but with a body like that, who cares."

Making deliveries around town, Smith continued to be the dull-witted hayseed. It helped him to know the town and its people. It also helped him spot the deadbeats, the chiselers and the slow payers that the Karen Freight Company was hauling for.

When these characters became difficult about money, Smith listened to their story, which was usually weak. Then he looked them straight in the eye as if he was going to break them in half and said, "Perhaps you would like to reconsider."

They saw serious trouble—or even death—and paid up on the spot.

After all, not many teamsters wore a gun tied low the way this one did, though most had rifles along. This man was wearing a gun tied low, and was known to be slow-witted as well. A spooky combination.

"Why, he might do anything."

They didn't know for sure. He might, could, did, and he already had in spades. For-

# Zero Smith

tunately for them, they had guessed right.

They paid up on the spot, cash on the barrel head and when they did, Smith went immediately into his act.

"Now suh, it wouldn't be proper for Miss Laura to have to wait for her money when she has always been straight with you, would it, suh.

"Ahm sure the child is most grateful, suh.

"Thank you kindly, suh, "Zero said, smiling that dumb grin and appearing to be as harmless as a puppy. The deadbeats, chiselers and "slow pays" were ashamed of themselves at first, but when Smith got through telling them how they were helping a poor young child just squeak through these difficult times and how grateful the Karen Freight Company was for their business, they began to swell with pride. Smith bowed before the people and said, "It was the Christian thing to do," climbed onto his wagon and piously drove away leaving each merchant or shipper wondering how he could have misjudged this poor, simple man and trying to figure how he could help the Karen Freight Company get more business.

By golly, it really was "the Christian thing to do."

None of them ever realized that they stood, for a very brief moment, on the edge of one of life's great precipices, yet many felt afterward that they were close to seeing their maker. Smith was not a murderer but he was very, very resourceful and he was very partial to the Karen Freight Company. He also, on occasion, looked these slow-pay people directly in the eye and appeared to them as if he might really be God's own avenger. Besides it was his job to see that Karen Freight came out on top.

Smith was to make several trips to near and far towns, but most of his deliveries were within fifty miles of Pinedale. Business picked up and there were no more deadbeats, much to Miss Laura's delight. Laura decided to keep an eye on her new teamster and check with her customers to see what they thought about the man. She was beginning to get the idea that there might be more to this newly hired hayseed than meets the eye.

During his third week, on another trip out of town, Smith again picked up a return shipment and a profit both ways. It was farm implements on the way out and bailed hay on the way back. Laura was very pleased and said so. She still thought there was more to this dull-witted hayseed than his first appearance implied but couldn't for the life of her put her finger on it. She thought there must be a side to him that didn't show, at least not yet revealed to her. Still Old John seemed to be right fond of Smith and she by now had asked some of her customers what they thought of the new driver. To a man, they all gave their approval of him. They said things like, "Seems honest enough and he is a good worker.

"A friendly sort though maybe a little slow in the smarts department but he seems to have a way with the team. His horses walk forward or back a step or two just with voice commands. I've never seen anything like it.

"Sometimes he has a look that seems dangerously evil but then he smiles and he seems very nice.

"I think he is looking out for your interests."

"Thank you," she replied.

Though she didn't say anything to anyone then, she made a mental note to study her new employee much more closely than she had since his arrival.

A few days later Laura felt compelled to ask Smith to discourage his friend, Candy, from coming around the freight office so often, saying, "It might be bad for business."

In fact she suspected that the very opposite was true. Every man in town was very much aware of Candy's obviously displayed, buoyant charms. What's more, if the truth be known, many of them had admired those same charms at very close range.

She was often followed to the freight office by men that just wanted to get to know her or say hello. On one or two occasions it resulted in new clients for the Karen Freight Company.

On more than one occasion Candy had personally ushered a smiling gent over to the freight office, saying that if he was shipping freight anyway, he really ought to help out the working girls of Pinedale.

Then she giggled and bounced her way out the door. The man was embarrassed and Laura was thoroughly mortified and speechless the first time it happened.

Later, Laura would put the men at ease by saying, "Candy is fond of one of our drivers and she wants business to improve so he can keep his job.

# Zero Smith

# CHAPTER FIVE

Not all of Zero Smith's trips for the Karen Freight Company were uneventful.

On one particular trip, just as Smith came around a hill, he was held up by three outlaws. They all had guns pointed at him but only one man looked like a professional. Smith tried to settle down the team.

"Let's have your money," shouted one of the outlaws. "Then we'll have a look at the stuff in those crates. Get down off that wagon."

That was his first mistake, and he never made another, because as Zero Smith jumped down he shot all three of them. Between the time Zero leaped from the wagon and the time he landed on the ground, all three bandits were dead. The fast gun first, and he was fast, and then the other two.

Smith calmly drove on into town, stopped to report to the sheriff that he found three bodies on the road and wondered if there was any reward for those fellows.

In answer to the sheriff's questions, he

said that he hadn't seen nor heard anything, that the three men were laid out when he came along, and their horses seemed to be scattered.

The only horse that Zero was able to catch without a rope was tied behind his wagon.

"I figure the horse is mine, sheriff, cause I found him and I want you to know, sheriff, that I took their gun belts because I didn't want any children that might come along to get a hold of them."

The sheriff had already marked Zero down as a near half-wit so he didn't press the issue.

"Put the horse in the freight company corrals and if no one claims him, he's yours. Same for the guns.

"Then unload and when you are done, I'll hire your wagon. You can help me haul the bodies back to town."

"Well now, sheriff, I'll have to get Miss Laura's permission before I can do that. These wagons don't roll less'n I have orders from the boss lady. That's one of the rules. Why sheriff, you ought to know that your own self. These wagons don't roll thout orders from Miss Laura. No Siree Bob."

The sheriff, who was nearly bored to death by the litany, could only stare at the ground in exasperation. To make matters worse for the sheriff, when Laura heard about it, she told Smith to take the day off and that she would send someone else along with the sheriff to do that dismal task. She did, but it took awhile.

In the meantime, Smith slyly suggested to Old John that while the sheriff was waiting for the wagon to be unloaded, John might ride out there with a rope and perhaps find two rather good horses. Smith added, "A large load of this kind was likely to take quite awhile to unload. Yes, indeed. Quite awhile."

An hour later Old John returned leading two horses and wearing a big grin.

The sheriff was more than somewhat puzzled when he found that all three outlaws were shot clean through the heart. When he returned to town he walked over to the freight office and asked to see Zero Smith's gun. Zero handed it to him by pointing the gun right at the poor man's eyes. The sheriff ducked and Zero apologized for being so clumsy.

Then Zero proceeded to drop his gun. He picked it up and handed it to the sheriff, butt first.

The sheriff smelled the gun and asked, "When was the last time you fired this gun, Smith?"

"I don't rightly know, but it's been a while. Why?"

# Zero Smith

"When did you clean it last?"

"Oh, I clean it all the time, sheriff. My daddy used to say 'a clean gun is a useful gun.'"

"That a fact!"

"Oh, yes sir, That's a fact, sheriff. He used to say that often. In fact I can still hear him saying it. Yes, sir, he'd say 'a clean gun is a useful gun.' He'd say that often."

The sheriff left, looking dour and thinking to himself that to ask a question of that half-wit was to tie himself up for an hour.

On another trip, Smith found that he was being followed by, of all things, a raven. He was just out of town when the raven flew to the nearest tall tree in front of the team. It squawked a few times and then flew on a short distance to always be in front of Smith. As the wagon came abreast of the bird, it would squawk again and fly further along the road. Smith reasoned this raven was smarter than the average bird as he had apparently figured a way to make a living without really working. Naturally, Zero Smith rewarded that kind of enterprise. He gave the bird more than half of his lunch, and that was more loot than any previous rider had ever given the great black bird.

From that moment on, the raven followed the generous teamster on all of his trips, no matter where he went, and Smith always fed the big bird.

The bird liked to roost in the high pines just back of the freight office. Old John had taken to feeding the bird, too. Needless to say, the bird became quite a conversation piece. People began to say, "Smith is the Karen Freight Company driver who always has a raven flying along. The bird follows that man every where. One time I saw them thirty miles from here."

Some folks said, "They're both bird-brained."

This line usually brought a few chuckles. Of course Smith knew nothing of this and wouldn't have cared even if he had.

It was some days before the great bird would land on the wagon while Smith was driving it. However, one day Zero Smith placed the food on top of the load and said, "Bird, you've known me long enough to have learned that you can trust me. If you want the food you'll have to land on the wagon to get it."

It wasn't long before the great black bird did land on the wagon. Smith was very pleased. The bird helped to make an otherwise dull trip rather pleasant.

One hot, muggy day, under leaden skies, Smith pulled into a desolate town that was on its last legs. The place was even dried up by western standards. He planned to spend

# Zero Smith

the night. He was unhitching his team when two of the town toughs, who were looking for some fun, saw the raven sitting on top of the load, and they walked over to the wagon.

"I've never liked those birds. They're scavengers and they live on carrion and other rotten things. I think I'll put a hole right through its eye."

Smith removed the thong from the hammer on his six-gun and faced both men.

"No, I don't think you will. Now let the bird alone and go on about your business."

One of the men, with a smirk on his face, said, "Our guns say we will."

"Not this time," answered Zero.

They were used to getting their way in this town. The two men made their dubious living by selling their guns. They were paid to intimidate farmers or push small ranchers from their land, burn a barn and even take a side in a range war. They sold their guns to the highest bidder.

A small crowd had gathered and the two gunslingers were bent on showing this yahoo with the bird that in this town they packed a whole lot of weight. They were going to show this bum just who he was dealing with and give everyone there a lesson in marksmanship.

"Fellas, I asked you once to leave the bird alone. Now I'm telling you, if you touch your guns I'll blow up your hands."

The crowd was seeking cover.

George, the tall one, spoke. "This clown thinks he can take us both."

Smiling with confidence he continued, "First we'll get him and then we'll get the bird."

They suddenly started to pull their irons and then they had a surprised look on their faces.

It seemed to everyone present that they heard only one shot, yet both men were standing there in shock with their guns on the ground, and their gun hands shattered and ruined for life.

The two men had seen some well known gunmen in the past, but never in their lives did they dream that anyone was as fast as the man they had just drawn against.

They were both shaken!

It was very quiet for a minute or two.

"No one's that fast," from a local.

"I don't believe it," said another.

"But there was only one shot." This came from a third witness.

"George and Slim certainly met their match this day, and that's something to celebrate," said a fourth man.

"We don't have to move out of the way for those two anymore. Come on, young fellow, you did this town a great service just now. Let me buy you a drink."

"Why, thank you, sir. That suits me right down to the ground, but first I want to say something to these good people."

Smith climbed up on the wagon and addressed the crowd.

"Folks, that there bird is the mascot of the Karen Freight Company. His name is "Raven" cause that is what he is, but I suspect he don't cotton to the name much cause when I call him he don't come. He does come if I whistle. He's freight company property now and I'm responsible for him just like the team and the wagon. I can't allow anything to happen to company property. Miss Laura said I was to take care of company property and I gave her my word on it, so naturally I couldn't let them shoot up Raven. Ya'all can see that, can't you?

"I did warn those fellas.

"You folks wouldn't want me to have to go back to my boss lady and tell her that someone in your town intended harm to the company mascot. Why, I might get fired."

These statements were greeted by much laughter.

The townspeople were incredulous. This hayseed teamster, who was still chewing on a straw, had taken out two good-for-nothing trouble makers, two of the town's fastest guns, and turned them into pussycats. And of all things, the quarrel was over a bird. In a split second, life in this town had improved.

The people were grateful, of course, but it was difficult for them to see why anyone would risk his life over a common raven, even if it was a company mascot.

Smith then climbed down off the wagon and strolled over to the two wounded men, who were on their way to see a doctor. He said to them, "I'm real sorry about all of this, but you know your own selves that I tried to talk you boys out of shooting that there bird.

"You fellas should never have put guns on in the first place. You didn't have the hands for it. Why, you were both slower than molasses in January. Take my advice and stay away from guns. You see, skillful gun handling is a gift from God, and when he was passing out that skill you boys must have been way out behind the barn.

"You're both lucky to have lived this long. Most gunmen would have put your lights out. It's lucky you met me cause I don't believe in killing."

The two men stood looking subdued in front of Smith, much like two delinquent children might stand before the headmaster of their school to get a scolding.

"Now go along and get patched up."

As the men walked away, they both knew deep down in their guts that they were lucky to be alive. They both knew they had just drawn on what must be the fastest gun alive. They also knew they were very vulnerable. They felt naked now and they were. Soon they would begin to realize their future was doubtful. The gun jobs which were their livelihood would dry up now, and over the years they had made many enemies. They would gradually realize it was time for them to find a hole and crawl in. A big deep one.

Smith went along to the saloon with the locals. The owner, a Scot, who was a tight fisted penny-pincher and witness to the shooting, announced, "The fust rrround is on the hoose."

Suddenly, it got so quiet they could hear a pin drop. Mouths gaped. Everyone stared at the man and at each other.

"Well, it tis," he said.

The locals whooped and hollered.

One man said, "I don't believe it."

Another said, "Two miracles in one day."

"Saints protect us," said a third as he crossed himself.

"Now that's real cause for celebrating."

"Angus buying drinks for the house. I never thought I'd live to see the day," from another.

They all laughed and bellied up to the bar.

As much fuss was made over the owner's

sudden generosity as was made over the shooting.

Smith drank for free but was very careful with liquor. He'd lived on the edge too long to be careless. When he spiraled out of the saloon to his team, it was part of his act.

Two locals, who were in worse shape than Smith appeared to be, tried to help him up on the wagon seat and they both fell down. One stayed where he was till morning. The other one crawled half way home and collapsed under a tree.

The hilarity continued through out the night. It was to be the bash of all time in this town. Later, the townspeople referred to the raucous celebration as the "Night of the Raven."

Around midnight, Smith took the harness off the team and put them in stalls in the livery stable. The owner of the livery stable was absent, still celebrating in the saloon. He was seen later crawling around over drunks on the saloon floor, looking for his glasses that had long since been crushed under a hundred heels.

When Smith crossed to the hotel, to his pleasant surprise there was a pretty lady in his bed. He started to apologize for being in the wrong room when she said, "This is your room sure enough and I'll leave if you really want me to."

# Zero Smith

She was drinking straight bourbon and poured him one. Smith picked up his glass and said, "Here's to friendship."

The lady was suddenly wearing a big smile on her face and she threw back the covers. Zero Smith could see she was very ripe all over. When he started to ask a question she put her finger to his lips and said, "Don't talk, just come to me."

He did and they did. Several times.

The saloon was a disaster. Not much was broken but most of the furniture was tipped over. Spilled glasses, ash trays, and spittoons with their accompanying horribles were strewn around the floor. There were people sprawled everywhere inside and out. Some were passed out on the porch. They had evidently started for home but didn't make it. A drunk was dangling, head down, on his back with one leg somehow tangled in one of the front steps. Those people leaving the place looked curiously at him, then stepped over him, but no one offered to help the man.

One dance hall girl was sleeping comfortably on a big table cushioning two drunks on her enormous breasts while her high heel was gouging the cheek of a third. A fourth man was using her ample backside for a pillow. He held her fleshy thigh with both hands and was wearing a big grin, even while asleep.

In the morning some of the serious drunks went out to breakfast and then returned to the saloon for a night cap, which for a very few just started them all over again. They were celebrating the fact that the drinks were free and that they were finally getting a "leg up" on old Angus who was out cold and loudly snoring right there before them in his own bar. They even thought the booze tasted better because they were drinking the best stuff in the house for free right in front of the sound asleep, tight fisted saloon keeper. The boozers were joined by others who saw a chance to get back at old Angus by proposing many toasts.

"To Scotland's greatest skinflint, who has finally seen the error of his ways."

"To Angus. May he sleep through another day or at least until we manage to drink his pub dry."

"To one of Scotland's own who finally sprung for a round. Bless him." And so it went until only a few were left standing.

Angus, the owner, was sleeping fitfully on his bar, and those few "diehards" still standing were still helping themselves to the free booze, which was very probably giving Angus bad dreams if not nightmares.

Yes, indeed. "The Night of the Raven" was to be fondly remembered as a celebration of major proportions. For Angus McClowd it was to be remembered as his worst nightmare. He swore that he was financially ruined. In fact, however, after that night, business became better than ever and he quickly recovered his losses.

When the story of the dispute over a raven got around the country, the freight business picked up. The shippers were all curious to see the famous raven and the slow thinking, fast gun, hayseed teamster.

With the new profits, Laura decided to have the buildings and wagons painted inside and out. She put the raven's image on the side of all of the wagons and over the front door of the company office. She even put the raven on the company stationary along with the slogan, "Deliveries as fast as the raven flies." Karen Freight was becoming prosperous, thanks to Zero Smith and the raven.

# CHAPTER SIX

Many days later, on a hot afternoon, Laura asked Smith to hitch up the buckboard. She came out, carrying a basket and looking as beautiful as ever. She was wearing a very low-cut, white peasant blouse and a long, white billowing full skirt. With her thick golden hair, she looked as fresh and pretty as a summer morning. This was quite a different image than the usual "look" of the boss lady when she was around the office.

Smith was pleased to see her looking this great as he stood by to help her into the wagon. He was about to hand her the reins when she said, "Smith, you're coming too."

"Yes, mam."

"And stop calling me mam."

"Yes, mam."

"Drive, will you, and if you say mam one more time I'll brain you with this basket."

Smith had a twinkle in his eye and Laura was annoyed. When she looked up at him and saw the laughter in his eyes, she became even more perturbed.

# Zero Smith

"Where to, mam, or should I call you Miss Laura"?

"Laura will do very nicely, thank you."

"In that case you can call me Zero."

"That's ridiculous. That's not a name. It's a number. Nobody has the name Zero. I'm going to call you Smith. Did your father have a sense of humor?"

"Would you mind telling me where we're going on this bright and glorious day, pretty lady?"

"You just stepped out of character and gave yourself away, Mr. Smith. I suspected there was more to you than this shuffling hayseed that I've been watching for several weeks."

Smith smiled but didn't say anything.

"You just drive west. I'll tell you when to pull off the road."

They traveled in silence for a while along a cool, shaded lane through a lush grove of tall cottonwood trees. The tree branches met overhead, and the ride through was very like a cool, dark tunnel, even though the sun peaked through here and there. The filtered light helped to make the many grassy areas seem like a park. It was a nice respite from the hot, dusty road as they left town.

Then Laura suggested, "It would be nice if one Mr. Zero Smith told his boss all about himself, starting with his most unusual name."

Smith was quiet for a while, as though he didn't know where to start.

He then began, "I came out of the war like so many men, with a few scars on my body and many scars on my soul. I wanted to be anonymous for a while, until I began to feel things again. I cared for nothing and no one. I was dead inside. I chose that name to remind me of what I had become."

"Just what had you become, Smith?"

"I saw myself as a kind of zero, a nothing, a nonentity. I was unfeeling, joyless, nothing made me laugh, I couldn't hold a job, I didn't like people, not even women for awhile, but I did get over that.

"The only thing I was good at was guns, but I didn't want anything more to do with killing, unless someone made me more angry than I already was. And I was angry, very angry, from the war. It all seemed such a waste. Good men on both sides left rotting on the battlefields. At night I had hideous nightmares about the war. I still do occasionally.

"The war was one long, horrible frustration. Nobody could win, nor did they, in my opinion. The cost was too great.

"After the war, I had a chip on my shoulder and I dared anyone to knock it off. I thought gunmen were vermin, myself in-

# Zero Smith

cluded, and the fewer of them around, the better for everyone. I challenged many men in those years.

" I was wired kind of tight in those days, so I was usually on the prowl and in trouble of one kind or another if I was around people. I had become dangerous to myself and to others. Too much anger and too quick with a gun. I made some enemies.

"I began to look for work that was more or less away from people. I took jobs such as line rider. I rode shotgun for the mines for awhile. Then I cowboyed up the Chisholm Trail a couple of times. I finally got to where I could hold a job. I've shot up a few men, all of whom deserved it, but I've never hired out my gun.

"A few months back I started to notice things in the natural world, things like a sunset or cloud formations, the sound of water falling over rocks in a brook and birds singing. Even the sound of insects. For years these things were lost to me.

"In time, I began to feel better about myself and I've been trying to avoid trouble. I have ridden away from some situations that a few years ago I would have jumped into with both feet, or perhaps I should say with both guns blazing.

"Lately I've calmed down and I thought I might be ready for a town job, and that's about the time I found you and the Karen Freight Company. Since I took this job, I've actually been enjoying it. I suspect it's because I look forward to coming to work each day, and that's because you're so nice to look at." Then he smiled.

When he did, it gave Laura a little burn deep down inside. She glowed on the outside as well and was annoyed with herself for being so transparent.

She thought him handsome. More than that, he was a man with a strange kind of power which she found fascinating. Very fascinating.

"Smith, that's the most you've talked in the six weeks you've worked for us."

"That's probably the most I've talked in the entire six years since the war."

"Go on, Mr. Smith."

"I think I'm on the mend now. I'm beginning to be at peace with myself more often these days and with the folks around me. I even enjoy getting up in the morning."

Laura was not aware that Smith was camping out in the nearby hills or along the stream and always, each night, in a different place. He also camped frequently with Candy at the hotel but saw no reason to mention that.

Nor did he mention the three holdup men he'd killed because he saw that situation as merely a neutral condition. The men were lawbreakers, and unlucky ones at that. They had drawn down on the wrong man.

Smith had always been a "heller" with a gun and since the war he had improved a lot, a whole lot.

"Since the war I have just drifted. I'm not a very pleasant person to be around, or at least I wasn't. I'm a lot better now than I was, but I still have a long way to go. That's about it."

They continued on their journey at a slow pace. The air was fresh after a recent rain. They were enjoying the day and the pretty wild flowers and, more important, they were enjoying each other. Zero was thinking to himself that this was the most pleasant thing that he'd done in recent memory, perhaps in years. Laura looked up at him with a smile on her face and just sighed. She was thinking along the same lines.

They had been following a stream for a mile or so, and as the stream left the road, Laura pointed to a little wagon trail that turned off and continued to follow the stream. Smith turned the horses and eased along for a quarter mile, with the tall grass getting so thick it brushed the sides of the rig. They had to protect their faces from some of it until they drove into a clearing, where Zero halted the horses.

Smith tied the horses and Laura got down and stretched. The place was very pleasant. There were big shade trees and lush short grass to lie on. They could hear the sound of the insects buzzing around and the stream drifting over a few rocks in the shallows. The sun was warm but not hot.

Smith sat down, resting his back against a large shade tree, and watched Laura set out the lunch. He enjoyed watching her. He liked the sun on her hair, the way she tilted her head when she talked to him, the way she moved her hands, and he particularly liked her ample bosom. She was indeed a beautiful woman.

"Before we eat, I would like to take a swim."

"So would I, but I didn't bring a swimsuit."

"Neither did I, Smith," and she promptly stood and began to undress right there in front of him.

Zero was astonished.

He watched and then watched some more. His eyes caressed her all over. She smiled, and seemed to like him looking at her. She was very matter of fact about removing her clothes, though secretly, she really did want his approval. She certainly got it.

"Woman, you are even more beautiful

than I imagined." And she was. She was certainly the most beautiful thing he had ever seen, and he told her so again.

She was slender, yet lush and ripe in all the right places. She had a high round backside and long, strong, graceful legs. Her breasts were high, round and large with small pink nipples. Even without support, her breasts curved almost as much above the nipples as they did below. Smith had never seen anything like them. They were perfect. She was perfect. The day was perfect. Zero Smith was wearing the biggest grin of his life.

Standing there in the buff, Laura took the pins from her hair and it cascaded well down below her shoulders. A large fold of honey colored hair fell across her breast and hung there provocatively.

"Now it's your turn," she said.

Zero, getting up off the ground and still wearing that big grin said, "Yes, mam."

Still smiling, he started to unbutton his shirt when Laura said, "Perhaps I'll do that for you one day."

"Little kitten, I sure hope so." Their eyes seemed to bore into one another. Smith hadn't felt this alive in a very long time. He continued to strip down. As he was taking off his gun belt, he subtly looked around to see if they were alone. He thought to himself, I may be in fairyland with a goddess, but this is still the real world. Being on his guard was too much a part of his makeup to allow him to be careless even for a few moments.

Once naked, he followed her to the water's edge. He was still carrying the gun and he placed it on the stream bank to keep it handy.

Laura made no specific advances toward him. Smith was taking his cue from her, and thought that perhaps she was just a tease.

She was partly coquette and partly just very natural. He could wait.

"Lady, I do like to look at you."

"I like to look at you, too," she said. "You're so well-muscled and lean. You're just beautiful."

She was so matter of fact about it, that Smith smiled. He liked the fact that Laura seemed comfortable with their nudity.

She went in the water slowly, squealing at the chilly water, while Smith dived in from the bank. The water was cool, refreshing and crystal clear. They both loved it. Laura went under, and when she came up Smith could see the chill bumps on her skin and her eye lashes were stuck together in little clusters by the water. Her hair was as slick as an otter's. She had the face of an angel and he

# Zero Smith

thought her exquisitely beautiful.

Laura was a complicated mixture of childish innocence, natural beauty, seductive woman and coquette, all in one person. She was subconsciously spinning a web for Zero Smith, with all the skill of a black widow spider. Like many a woman before her, she was responding to her animal-like instincts. She had moved before Smith with rather finely honed seductive skills, of which even she was unaware. Now in the water she was doing the same thing.

His thoughts ran on. "This little lady has my head spinning and that means trouble in any man's language. On top of that, she is my boss. He remembered words his father used to say, 'One sure way to lose a job is to get too chummy with the boss.'"

Smith allowed that perhaps his father had never worked for anyone who looked as pretty as this little coquette.

It had been a long time since Zero Smith had been swimming with a lady. He wasn't sure yet how this wonderful event had come about. One day he was the slow-witted hostler and driver, and the next he was elevated to an escort of a fair maiden. Apparently she had seen through him, at least enough to question his role. He wasn't worried that others might see through his disguise. Laura and Old John were the only people with whom he had any real contact. When they went back to town, Smith would put on his act as the dull-witted driver just as easily as putting on his coat.

As for now he couldn't be more pleased with himself and his present company. Here in fairyland he was happy. The real world would come crashing down soon enough.

They swam some more, yet neither one made any advances toward the other. They swam underwater together, partly to look at the bottom and to look at each other. They let the current carry them down a short ways, then swam back against the slow meandering stream. It was just good fun. Finally Laura suggested, "Let's get out."

They lay on the lush warm grass in the sun to dry. Afterward, they dressed, and as Laura prepared lunch, she continued with her questions.

"Smith, why do you have enemies? You seem nice enough."

He considered being vague, elusive or just outright untruthful, but felt she was too important for that, so he answered her bluntly.

"Because I've killed some men and they always seem to have friends or relatives. Not just during the war, but since then as well."

"Do you have the reputation of a gunman?"

# Zero Smith

"Yes, I suppose I do."

"Well, I don't care. I like you just the way you are. Please don't tell me any more about it. How long do you plan to work for us?"

"I don't know. When I started it was just something to do. I wanted to work at something that was constructive. Something physical that would allow me to stretch my muscles and replenish my brain with good and pleasant thoughts, and to forget the war. If I have many days like this one, I'll be human again in no time, thanks to you, pretty lady."

"In that case I'll see to it, but for now, let's eat. I just have a few things to do and the food will be ready."

"While you're doing that, I'll water the horses and let them graze."

As Zero unhitched the horses and led them down to the stream, he found himself wondering about his lady-boss. What could he contribute to her life, even if he wanted to? He had already made a mess of his first life, as he called it, and now, living under the cloud of being a gunfighter, he was rapidly making a mess of his second life as Zero Smith.

He chose the name of Smith to be anonymous, and the name of Zero because after the war he felt like a zero. This new boss of his had awakened all kinds of feelings in him that he thought were dead. He felt protective of her, but at the same time her provocative behavior had awakened another facet of his personality. The Candys of the world were well remembered, but this was different. Very different indeed.

As for Laura, protection he would give her freely. Regarding his other interests in this Olympian goddess, it would require iron discipline just to keep his job, unless of course, she chose to rape and pillage him. In that case, he would be a very willing victim indeed.

He looked up from his reverie to see her studying him. Their eyes met and they held one another with a longing look.

Smith thought to himself, this little kitten is ten years younger than I am, and a thousand years younger in living. The generous move for him was to go on down the road. He was not dead inside any more, but he knew deep down that he wasn't very far from it. He still had a very quick flash point. He was dangerous. He was trouble. At least, he always had been. He felt that she deserved a better person than himself. Perhaps in time.

Many times in the past he had considered taking another identity and had a few times. He could still wear a gun, but with a

# Zero Smith

new name he wouldn't be called out by gunhawks trying to build their reputations.

Zero Smith was famous, deceptively so. Of late, people said, "He just doesn't look like a fast gun." His manner was quiet, deliberate, slow moving and kind. He liked horses and children and was kind to old folks. In a nutshell, Zero Smith was a model citizen, except of course at gun time. Then he became a devil.

Laura was doing a little thinking of her own. She was wondering about her feelings for this man and why she had asked him to drive her out here in the first place. She was attracted to him before she discovered that he had a good mind, and now she was more attracted than ever. Now she was looking at him seriously and for the first time really closely. She liked what she saw.

Seeing him in the all-together had really started her emotions to dance around. She thought him beautiful all over, which was why she swam away from him. It was more than that. It was more than a physical attraction. There was something elusive about him, something that she couldn't quite define. But she felt that it was very important and powerful, like an aura similar to what the Cheyenne Indians called their "Personal Spirit", or their "Personal Totem."

Zero Smith certainly had a personal

"spirit" about him, and she hoped it would be kind to her. Perhaps in time she would discover what the Zero Smith spirit really was.

Laura finished arranging a picnic lunch for them on a blanket in a nice grassy spot in the shade next to the stream. In the center of the blanket was a glass filled with wild flowers. There were daisies and some blue flowers he didn't know. He liked them. He thought them a nice touch and he told her so.

Smith sat on the blanket to eat.

"A gunman who likes flowers? You are a complex man, Mr. Smith."

Laura was placing the food on the plates and asked him if he wanted coffee or wine or both.

"Both, thanks, but the wine first if you don't mind."

They ate in silence for awhile, and then Laura asked, "Have you ever been married?"

"No," he said, simply.

She thought she saw him look back in time, as though lost to her, for a moment.

Then he looked up at her and smiled. She smiled back at him, feeling great.

They finished lunch and stretched out on the blanket. It was cool and Smith observed the moving shadows on Laura's face made by the dancing leaves in the filtered

# Zero Smith

light.

"Let's visit," she said.

"I thought we were."

"Well, for me, visiting is when we talk about all kinds of things so that we really get to know each other. Most men don't know how to visit, particularly here in the west. Why some of them are practically nonverbal. If I had a man, I'd want to be able to talk to him and I would want him to be a very good listener. You seem to listen rather well, but you don't offer much about yourself."

"Pretty lady, until today there was no need, and not only that, I didn't think anyone was interested."

"That has all changed now because I'm interested, very much so, so tell me all about yourself."

"Yes, mam," he said smiling.

"Oh, you!" and she rolled over and put her head in his lap.

"If you leave anything out I'll fire you."

Smith was propped up against a tree looking down at her. He was about to touch her hair, when out of the corner of his eye he saw a bright sun reflection where there shouldn't be one. Simultaneously he grabbed Laura and his gun as he rolled both of them down a slope to a small depression against the stream bank, just as a rifle bullet

TWANGED a scar on the tree where he had been sitting.

When Zero saw the bullet scar, he knew the direction of the shooter. He also realized that the shooter had them pinned down, and that the maverick could circle around behind them if he chose to without their seeing him. He could then pick them off at his leisure. In a word, they were "sitting ducks."

Smith had only one chance, a slim one to be sure, but it was the only move he had. He snapped off two shots in the direction of the metallic reflection and was rewarded when he heard the shooter cry out. It had been a very lucky shot. The bushwhacker cried out, "You've killed me, I'm gut shot."

Still Smith stayed down, and he held Laura down under him. The shooter could be lying. He waited a while, and then slid off to investigate. Sure enough, he found the man more dead than alive. The bullet apparently ricocheted off his rifle and then plowed a wide furrow through him, and exited out his right side just below the last rib. It was an awful wound.

"Why did you shoot at me? I don't know you."

"You're either very good, or awful lucky," said the dying man.

"Who are you?" Smith asked.

"It don't matter now."

# Zero Smith

"Why were you gunning for me?"

"There will be more coming for you," he said. Then he died.

Smith pondered the man's words. Perhaps Zero's reputation had caught up with him. Few people actually knew what the famous Zero Smith looked like. Perhaps he was a look-alike for some other fast gun. He vowed to walk "Injun" soft and be fox careful until he learned the whole story.

Zero took a second look at the dead man, covered the wound with the man's hat, and then summoned Laura to have a look.

"Do you recognize him"?

"No, I don't know him."

Riding back in the wagon Smith asked Laura if she knew of anyone who would want to kill her.

"No, I have no enemies. The freight company had a few slow payers until you came along, but I don't know of anyone that would want to harm me."

# CHAPTER SEVEN

When they returned to town, Zero reported the incident to the sheriff and smiled about his outrageously lucky shot.

Later the sheriff mentioned that it seemed like a mighty big hole for just one bullet.

"Big huh, well the varmint deserved it, shooting at Miss Laura that away."

"You didn't tell me that."

"You didn't ask me, sheriff."

"Well, if that don't beat all. If I'd known that I'd a helped you shoot the S.O.B. This town thinks mighty highly of Miss Laura."

"Yes, sir."

Smith, back in his slow-witted role, stared at the ground and answered in his vacuous way. He walked away mumbling to himself, knowing full well that the sheriff was watching him. Perhaps he was overdoing it, but it didn't hurt to continue to dull the light of his already dim-witted reputation.

Zero suspected the back-shooter might

be wanted in a few places, and if the sheriff earned his keep, it was just possible there was some reward money lying around somewhere. He would ask about that in the morning. He did and there was. Five hundred dollars worth of "lying around" reward money.

The sheriff had to do all the dirty work, go and get the body, identify the dead man and then pay five hundred dollars to the near nitwit, Smith.

He did all of those things, but very reluctantly. When he was finished, he was sure he was in the wrong business.

Karen Freight Company got the hauling job for the dead man. Smith got the reward. He also got the outlaw's horse and guns, the undertaker got to bury the man at the county's expense, and the sheriff got all of the work. He had to drive the wagon both ways over a very dusty road and he got a sore back from lifting the corpse. He also got his clothes stained from some of the horribles in the dead man's innards. When the sheriff returned to Pinedale, people shunned him because he smelled about as bad as the corpse.

It was not the sheriff's best day.

# CHAPTER EIGHT

Miles to the east, two riders looked across some small rolling hills and saw a farmhouse, a tired barn and some out buildings. None of the buildings had seen paint in years. It was difficult to tell if they had ever been painted. The place was set back among large shade trees and some willows that grew along a small creek. It was a difficult place to approach without being seen.

The riders' immediate interest was in getting water for their canteens and their horses. That is, until they saw a flaxen haired woman carrying a bucket toward a back shed. It appeared to them that she was about to slop the hogs or perhaps feed the chickens.

The riders waited. Soon the woman returned to the house and went inside.

The riders kneed their horses down the road toward the house. The younger one elbowed the other and grinned, but neither of them said anything because the younger of the two was a mute, and the older one wanted to take the lady by surprise, if possible.

That wasn't likely because most ranches had a dog or two. He reasoned it would be right neighborly of her to share some of the creek water and maybe a meal for the two hungry and thirsty travelers. Wrong.

They kept watching. It was unusual not to see a man around, and as yet the dog hadn't made a sound. Likely they were both out hunting or on some errand and would come back at any time.

After watching the place for a long while, they rode down to the house.

"Hello the house!"

"What do you want?" It was a deep resonant voice, but definitely female. It came from inside the house.

"We would like to water our horses and fill our canteens."

"I have a rifle pointed at your belt buckle. You can water downstream and then be on your way."

"We was hoping you might be a little more friendly and maybe fix us some grub. We'll be glad to do some chores for you. Josh here is plumb wore out."

She could see they were both on the sorry side, with worn out gear and dirty clothes. The men had no possessions and their horses were just hide over bones. The older one, who was doing all the talking, had matted hair and dirty teeth.

The sooner they were gone the better. She wasn't afraid exactly, just uneasy. Well, she had a good rifle and she could hit a squirrel's eye at a good distance.

"Well, you're out of luck. Now move on down the stream and water where I can see you. If you come back this way I'll nick your ears first, and if that don't do it, I'll shoot both of you."

Josh couldn't speak but there was nothing wrong with his hearing. He was already scared and he grabbed the sleeve of his older brother and began to pull him back toward the road.

The older brother, Ben, was beginning to take a dim view of this not so friendly treatment.

"Now hold on there, mam. You got no call to treat us this way." Anger was in his voice.

TWANG. The bullet ricocheted from a tree beside his head.

"The next one will nick your ear.

Josh put spurs to his horse and hightailed it.

Ben broke into a sweat and trotted his horse down to the stream. They were still within rifle range, particularly if that was the kind of rifle that he guessed it to be, a .50 caliber Hawken. He thought to himself, I'll

# Zero Smith

bet that thing shoots a mile. He was almost right. It depends on who's making the loads.

Ben reasoned that this was no fair damsel in distress. If she had put that bullet on the tree next to his head on purpose, then she could really shoot, probably better than most men. She could certainly shoot much better than he could, and as for Josh, the only time he strapped on a gun, he had shot himself in the foot.

Ben was beginning to think that he and Josh were not cut out for this outlaw life. It had started out well enough, living off the land, which meant stealing chickens, and a calf now and then. They had even been highwaymen a few times, robbing a few old folks. However, the further west they had come, the more cantankerous everyone seemed to be. Out here they all carried guns, even some of the women, and they all were better shots than he was.

They stole a few chickens from a farmer one afternoon, and as they were riding away, the farmer shot away Josh's saddle horn.

Josh had the shakes for the next two days just thinking about how close that shot had been to his manhood.

Josh, the mute, had written, "Why, Ben, I couldn't get a girl then could I, Ben?"

"I suppose not, Josh, but then you ain't never had one anyway."

Josh sulked for two more days.

Now they had called on "The Queen of Female Sharp-Shooters" and Josh was beginning to have doubts about his older brother's smart box. It was all very confusing. What the whole thing amounted to was that Josh couldn't speak and Ben couldn't think very well.

Ben decided that if they didn't find a new partner soon that could do both, then they would just have to give up outlawing and go to work. The very thought of work made them both uneasy.

Ben vowed to give outlawing one more try. He knew about the Karen Freight Company and heard that the wagons were frequently driven by an old black man. He figured it would be easy to hold up the wagon, then go through the stuff and maybe find guns or money, or who knows what? Wrong.

They tried to hold up Zero Smith. They had the right company but the wrong driver.

Ben shouted," Put up your h...."

Smith shot up the young man's gun hand and then noticed that the other one didn't even have a gun.

Ben was howling with pain, and Josh's face was contorted with fear, but he made no sound.

"You ain't a black man."

"What's wrong with this fellow?" Zero

said looking at Josh.

"He's my brother and he can't talk."

"Well, young fellow, you're much too slow to have a gun job and now you're through shooting anything for a good long while. You fellows climb down. I don't take kindly to folks that try to hold up the Karen Freight Company. I want you to remember that I just saved your life. I could just as easily have killed you. Another man probably would have.

"Now follow me. We're going back to that farm and see if anyone there can bandage your hand. Then I want you two to report to the sheriff in Pinedale. You tell him I sent you, and wait there till I return. My name's Smith.

"You tell him that you shot yourself while cleaning your gun. Now, if you do this I'll see to it that you don't go to jail. If you don't see the sheriff, I'll hunt you down. I'm a fair hand with one of these. Smith shucked his iron and shot the left boot heel off of each rider.

They were both so scared that Ben said, "Yes, sir!" And the mute nodded vigorously.

"Put your rifle in the wagon and leave the hand gun. It's useless now. From the look of it, it was junk before I shot it up. Mount up and follow me."

They rode back to the farm.

Smith "helloed" and waited at a respectable distance.

TWANG. A rifle bullet ricocheted from a stump near the team.

This got Zero's attention.

"Hold on there. I'm with the Karen Freight Company and I have a wounded man here. He needs some bandaging, till he can get to a doctor. It's a long way to town."

A deep feminine voice said, "You come up to the house, and leave those two where they are."

Smith looked at Ben who by this time was hurting a whole lot.

"I'll see if I can get some bandages."

Smith drove the wagon, including the rifles, on up to the house, climbed down and introduced himself.

"Howdy, mam. My name is Smith and I drive for the Karen Freight Company in Pinedale," Zero said, while tipping his hat to the lady.

"I came across these two fellows and one of them has shot himself in the hand. I was wondering if you have anything to bandage it with.

"I suppose it's the Christian thing to do, but those two came by here earlier today and were too pushy to suit me. They acted like they were going to take what they wanted, so I ran them off."

# Zero Smith

"They're mighty humble now, mam. Neither of them is armed, and one is carrying a whole lot of hurt."

"I'll just get some iodine and something to wrap the wound."

As they walked back to where the young men were, Smith noticed that the woman was attractive. She still had not given her name and he didn't ask. Her farm was on the tired side and so were her clothes, but she looked first-rate. She had long, blonde hair with beautiful sun streaks in it. Her skin was tanned, and she had a well endowed body. Like most western women, she seemed to have a capable manner.

When Zero and the lady arrived, they found Ben on the ground, seated Indian fashion, holding his hand to his chest and moaning. The bleeding had slowed remarkably because the hole was straight through. There were splinters in his hand from the shattered walnut grips.

The lady first pulled out all of the small wood pieces that she could find. Then she poured iodine right into the hole. When she did, Ben went straight up in the air. When he came down he fainted, and she dressed the wound skillfully.

When he became conscious, Ben was sure she had poured all of that stuff in the wound just for spite. He was not grateful.

Smith guessed that this lady had dressed bullet wounds before.

"He should see a doctor as soon as he can."

"Yes, that's just what he will do. I intend to take them into town and get that one fixed up. They sure are a sorry pair. Kinda down on their luck. Apparently the younger one has his problems, too. He's a mute. You don't by any chance need a strong back around here do you?"

"I sure do need some help, but I can't afford to pay anyone."

"Who said anything about paying? The way I figure it, the younger one isn't likely to misbehave as long as we keep an eye on Ben. Josh can work for you while the other one mends. I believe that I can put them up in the stable at the freight office. Josh can ride out in the morning and give you a hand. He can read and write. Just write out what you want him to do each day."

Smith turned his attention to the two men. "Josh, give your brother a drink of water and then help him on his horse."

Smith and the woman talked as they returned to the house. She agreed to give Josh a try for a few days. It was decided to work him away from the house so she could keep an eye on him.

Smith mounted the wagon and said,

# Zero Smith

"Much obliged, mam. I'll look in on Josh in a day or two."

On the way back to town, Zero Smith made it very clear to the brothers what was expected of them, and they reluctantly agreed.

Smith further pointed out that they were probably the world's worst outlaws, and that they were lucky to find out in time to change the course of their lives. They were equally lucky to have found the right person to help them along the road to honesty, though the brothers weren't all that sure of it at the time.

Ben said, "You mean I'm working for that woman who helped me?"

"No, Ben. I mean you're working for me. I'm going to ride herd on you fellows for a while. Then I'm going to put you to work as cowhands."

"We don't know anything about being cowhands."

"You will, and if you work out I'll even pay wages and room and board."

Josh was nodding vigorously again. He made some hand signs to Ben that implied that it was better than jail.

The fact was that no one had ever given these two the time of day. It was the best and only deal they had ever been offered in their entire lives. They accepted with humble resignation and a whole lot of fear.

# CHAPTER NINE

The boys had come west from a shack in the Tennessee hill country where the soil raised rocks and their father raised welts on their backs.

Their father was a brutal man. He was old and thin and worn out long before his time, just like his farm. The rocks of his hillside farm had won. He gave up on crops except corn, which he used to make a fairly good moonshine, but he was his own best customer. When he drank, his disenchantment with life made him mean.

The boys figured that any place would be better than where they were, and it was.

After the boys left, their pa transferred his wrath to the hounds, until they, too, ran off. The mean, bitter, old man was left with moonshine and fleas, which is about what he deserved.

When the boys left home, they found it was better than being back on the rock farm except that they were frequently hungry. Of course they had been frequently hungry at

93

home, too. Neither of them had anything except the clothes on their backs. There was one pair of shoes between them and they each had a knife and the oldest, Ben, had a flint. They could build a fire. They had a tough time getting enough odd jobs because neither of them knew how to work. They'd spent most of their boyhood watching the cooker at their father's still.

If it blew up, he beat them. But then, he sometimes beat them when it didn't blow up, or for no reason at all. Usually he beat them just because he felt like it. It was a workable system for the old man until the boys grew too big to put up with their pa. Josh was twice as strong as the old man, but didn't know it until one day when he stopped his father's hand in mid air. Instead of receiving a blow, he crushed his father's fist in his own hand. From that time on, his pa never attempted to strike the boys again.

Ben thought every father beat his sons, but was damn tired of it and he was ready to leave long before the confrontation between Josh and their father. He wasn't sure what to do next but he knew they should do something and do it quick. That night Josh pulled on Ben's sleeve until they were both away from the house. Then Josh conveyed his idea to Ben of going west, and they just walked away. After being hungry for a few days, they decided to become outlaws and steal whatever they needed.

They started by stealing chickens, then an old beat up rifle, and ended by stealing horses. They weren't even any good at that. The nags they were riding were the only ones they had stolen and they had done the rightful owners a big favor by taking them off their hands. The pistol Ben used in his attempt to hold up Smith was junk, as Zero guessed, even before he shot it up.

They certainly were a sorry pair.

Smith looked at them and just shook his head. He doubted if there was even a warrant posted for their arrest. He assumed, and rightly, they weren't even good enough to be bad enough to have earned a warrant for their arrests being posted.

Smith wondered how the pair had made it this far west. When he asked them, they didn't know they were "this far west."

"How far west are we?"

Smith just shook his head.

When they got to Pinedale, Smith found the doctor and left Ben in his care while he and Josh went to the freight office.

Zero had some explaining to do, but Laura went for the idea of Smith helping the boys, as long as Smith accepted the responsibility for them.

Smith reasoned that as long as Ben was

# Zero Smith

hurting, he would be easy to keep an eye on, and Josh wasn't apt to go very far without his older brother. They both had a bleak future to look forward to if someone didn't give them a hand. Smith was rather surprised at himself. Just a few weeks back he would not have even noticed their plight, yet here he was giving two troublesome strangers a helping hand. It even made him feel good, though he wasn't quite sure why.

Later the same day Smith went to the land office to see what was for sale. To his surprise, there were two adjacent properties available at a fair price. Both properties had huge, good quality grasslands and plenty of water the year round. There were large timber tracts, rolling hills, some valleys and small streams everywhere. Some of the country on the ranches was up high. Tomorrow, he would take a several day look at these ranches.

After Ben was fixed up, Smith took both of the young men to the best restaurant in town and gave them their first good meal in a long, long time, perhaps in their entire lives. He told them that he was going to buy a ranch and they were going to help him start it.

He explained further that he would hire a cook and buy some cows and a few good horses and that as he didn't want to quit his job with the freight line just yet. He was willing to put the boys in charge of the place. They could run it as if it was their own so long as they behaved themselves and followed his orders. He further explained that he would look in on them frequently just to be sure they were doing all right.

The downside to all of this was that if they refused, Smith was going to turn each of them over to the sheriff and they could do about five years in prison. The boys agreed, with the understanding that it included Josh working for the nice lady for a week or two until Ben was healthy enough to work.

Smith explained that he would buy something around here, and when the purchase was finalized the boys would come to work for him. He explained to them that they wouldn't have to do all of the thinking because he intended to hire additional cowhands and an experienced man to be the ramrod.

# Zero Smith

# CHAPTER TEN

The next day Zero rode out to have a look at the two ranches. Each one had just about everything any rancher could have wanted, and the land agent was sure that Mr. Smith would want one or the other. He thought the price a bit high on each of them, but the owners were sure that the properties were worth it. After having a several day close look at each of them, Zero said, "I'll take it."

The agent asked? "Which one?"

"Both."

"Both?"

"Both."

"Mr. Smith, do you really have that kind of money?"

Zero Smith did indeed have that kind of money. The money was under another name in his former life. He was the heir apparent to a vast financial network. The family corporations included banks, commercial real estate and shipping companies, plus several manufacturing plants.

"Will you accept a check drawn on the

# Zero Smith

Wells Fargo Bank of San Francisco?"

The agent smiled the biggest smile of his life.

Smith used his saddle for a desk and promptly wrote the check for the correct amount. He held the check away from the land agent. Then he explained that he didn't want the transaction known just yet, and swore the man to secrecy. He requested that the land agent tell no one of the deal for at least two months.

Smith agreed not to take possession until the check had cleared the bank. The agent said it would take only a few days because they could do it by telegraph.

The check cleared and the deeds were recorded in due time. Smith owned a ranch, and it was registered, and so was the new brand. It was to be the "0" Brand. The 0 Brand would be eight inches high and be placed on the left shoulder of his cattle and four inches high and on the right hip of the horses.

When the deal closed, Smith went to the next town's blacksmith and asked him to make six branding irons in each size. He bought horses and other supplies. He requested the supplies be shipped by the Karen Freight Company. He delivered the supplies himself, with the help of the boys.

Ben was still hurting, but he tried to help

out. Josh was actually enthusiastic about their new adventure.

All of these goings on were kept secret from everyone except Old John. He enjoyed being privy to the secret and thought it would be a great joke on Laura if she discovered her freight driver was indeed a very wealthy man.

Smith outfitted Old John with several bottles of good whiskey and said, "This is so I don't wear out my welcome. Maybe sometime you can share your 'cottonwood music' with me." Zero's curiosity, about just what Old John's music was, prompted him to invite himself to hear it.

John smiled and said, "It would be a pleasure to have you hear my 'cottonwood music." You come anytime. I'll save some of this whiskey for you if you don't take too long."

Smith set the boys to mending fences, and generally getting the places ready for livestock.

Some cattle were purchased through an agent in the next town and delivered to the Zero ranch quietly, without any fuss. The money arrived by wire from San Francisco, so the locals figured that someone from that city was the new owner.

The Zero ranch was operational. The boys were becoming sure enough cowboys, and they liked it. Their job was mostly to keep the stock grazing in certain areas. They practiced roping on stumps and fence posts. Smith told them to stay at it till their hands were raw. As Ben's gun hand was the wounded right one, and still healing from the gunshot, he learned to rope with his left hand.

Zero bought them outfits, from hats to spurs, and cleaned them up. He insisted they wash their faces and hands and brush their teeth daily, bathe at least twice a week and wash their clothes weekly.

They were riding better horses than anything they had ever ridden. Their clothes, personal gear and saddles were much better than anything they'd ever had before.

They were beginning to look like cowhands and even more important, they were beginning to feel and think like cowhands.

Smith hired repairmen from town, through Old John, to spruce up the ranch buildings and to haul away the junk that had accumulated over the years. The stuff seems to pile up on every ranch. The clean up was contracted to the Karen Freight Company to be hauled away and disposed of.

From one place it went out by the wagon load. Dead this and rusty and broken that, all loaded by town men and then taken away. This allowed Zero Smith to oversee the job from behind the scene and still give Laura's company a little extra business.

# Zero Smith

Smith had to make a similar deal with the local banker that he had made with the real estate man. If he wanted the account, he was to be sworn to secrecy for a few weeks.

Zero chose the better of the two ranch houses to set up his ranch headquarters. When the job was done, it looked like a whole new outfit.

Smith gave a diagram to Old John showing where he wanted trees planted. Then Old John had the men plant accordingly. The trees were mostly of the deciduous type, but there were many evergreens as well. All of the trees were good sized so the folks wouldn't have to wait long for them to give shade. They were placed against or near the work buildings to provide shade in the summertime, but also to display the fall colors. They even planted shade trees for the horses near one of the larger corrals. Others were planted near the stream in front of the main house. Still others were placed along the stream to create a cool, shaded, parklike place.

The other ranch house was several miles away and would be used only on occasion when the men were working that part of the now combined ranches. The two ranch houses were located on the same beautiful, wide, meandering creek, so there was ample water at each place.

The grasslands were well watered. They

# Zero Smith

were laced with many small creeks that came from the snow fields to the north.

The new 0 Ranch was rich in timber and grassland. In addition to the natural snow melt run off, the summer had been unusually rainy and the high hills were beautifully green. Even the south slopes were green. The surrounding country looked like a fairyland.

The wind waved the rich, green, grass on the broad valley floor, and on the higher ground there were great meadows of grass and wild flowers along with many kinds of trees.

The evergreens were mostly pine, several kinds, plus cedar and juniper. There were aspen, vine maple and always along the creeks were cottonwood and willow.

The timbered places would be tough to chase cows and impossible to do any roping.

Zero thought maybe the answer was dogs. He put Ben to inquiring about buying a dozen good cow dogs. This proved to be very difficult as they found that few ranchers used herd dogs at this time. Smith shelved the idea for the time being, knowing he could have some shipped in from Australia if necessary. In the meantime, he would buy whips and have his men learn the whip. A whip could help to move cattle on open ground, but it was nearly useless in the high brush or thick timber.

# Zero Smith

Smith considered hiring sawyers to thin the trees in some of the more densely forested areas one day. Perhaps he might start a small wood business. Corral poles and fire wood. If he employed the boys on it a few hours a day it would help to toughen them up. Perhaps in a few weeks when Ben's hand was better. As Smith began looking around the ranch he saw the possibility of starting several small businesses. Lumber, perhaps selling hay, and he thought there might even be a possibility of minerals here. All in due time. Smith was surprised to find himself thinking like the businessman that he once was before the war.

# Zero Smith

# CHAPTER ELEVEN

Josh had worked with the farm lady for three weeks and learned to like her. He also learned that her name was Mary Hightower, that she was a recent widow and that her farm was going broke. When Josh returned to the Smith place, he reported his findings by writing on the small pad he always carried.

Zero rode out to have a look at her place the next day. He knew that her property bordered on his on one side and that the small stream was the other border, a branch of which ran just in front of her house. He thought to himself that his neighbor lady should be raising cattle. The place was plenty big enough and though there was some forest sprinkled around here and there, it was mostly open meadow and large grass areas like his own place.

Her house was the only one around that had a cold water faucet in the kitchen. It was the first thing her husband had done for her when they moved west to the "farm." They

# Zero Smith

called it a farm when in fact it was really a sizable ranch.

As Mary Hightower was the nearest neighbor to Smith's place and an attractive woman besides, the hands all kept an eye out for her and, in fact, did get "to see her" on occasion. Even from far off it helped to make their day. The only thing better was a trip to town where there were many women to look at and a few whores to play with.

One day Mary rode by and said to Zero, "I never would have believed that these two could amount to anything, but they seem to have taken hold so far."

"It might be a little soon to judge," Smith said.

"Perhaps, but I watched them one day when they didn't know I was around. They worked well enough."

"Yes, I've watched them also and I'm pleased so far," said Zero. He continued, "Which reminds me. They really don't have enough to do just yet and I was wondering if you would allow us to run some of our cattle on your graze. I would be glad to pay you for it, either in dollars or in cattle. The boys can keep them out of your crop areas."

"I think that would be all right Mr. Smith. In fact, I think that would be just fine," she said with a great big smile.

Smith thought to himself that his first

payment to her would be in dollars to help her get on her feet, and after that she could begin to accept cattle as payment. He didn't tell the widow that he had more than enough grass to feed his cows on his own range at this time. He told the boys that it was better to save his grass for later when they would have more cows, which was to be sooner than they expected.

One morning Pinedale awoke to see a thousand head of cattle going by just west of town, accompanied by about a dozen cowhands, a remuda of some very good looking horses and a chuck wagon that was pulling another wagon loaded with supplies.

Rumors ran wild, and people said things like, "It all belongs to some wealthy Easterner."

"What has the widow been up to?"

"That country will feed ten times that many cattle."

"Who bought the old Ames' place next to the widow Hightower?"

"I saw that Ben fellow, you know the one with the wounded hand, moving cows on to the Hightower place."

"Sheriff, what's going on out there?"

Old John had heard some of this and filled Zero in when he showed up for work. Zero simply smiled and took charge. Many of the townsfolk thought he was to be the

# Zero Smith

new foreman. They watched and wondered. They talked and gossiped. Rumors flew left and right. Zero, totally ignoring all of the flack, went about his business as driver for the Karen Freight Company while gradually putting together a cow ranch.

He met the herd boss and rode out to the ranch with his new cattle. The herd was a mix of everything. There were Longhorn, quite a few Hereford and some wild Mexican stuff that was left over from the days of the Spanish explorers. Mostly they were younger cows, many with calves, about sixty bulls and some steers which he planned to sell in the fall along with the culls.

His main problem now was to find some riders to look after this stuff. The new stock was placed on lush grass along the stream, and they weren't likely to go anywhere. The Mexican stuff was mostly steers, which was all right with Smith because he wanted to upgrade his herd over the next few years. All of the these smaller critters would have to go.

The boys could move the cattle back along the creek if they scattered, giving Smith time to find and hire more men. He planned to ask in every town as he made his deliveries for Karen Freight Company. Smith was able to find one or two men. Now and then they showed up for work.

# CHAPTER TWELVE

When the crew increased, it became necessary to hire a cook instead of the men taking turns preparing grub. Smith found the task more difficult than he imagined. He placed ads in some of the eastern news papers with no luck. Not every cook wanted to live on a remote cattle ranch way out in the Wyoming territory. Once again he consulted Old John.

Much to Smith's delight, John thought he might know of someone. The two men discussed the problem over whiskey at the Karen Freight Company's corrals late one afternoon after work. The young man that John had in mind to be cook had an uncle by the name of Franco who was a Mexican hiding out in the Territory and working the loading dock of a feed store in Pinedale. Old John had whiled away many an hour with the man over whiskey and only recently heard of the plight of Franco's nephew and his girlfriend.

The two young Mexicans were hiding here in the territory, having come from a

# Zero Smith

large rancho in old Mexico that ran along the Texas border. The nephew was hiding from his patron because he had taken a girl who was promised in marriage to the patron's son. The young man and the girl had been sweethearts since childhood and she did not care for the spoiled son of the patron. To avoid the marriage, they had run away together. To escape the patron and his men was no small accomplishment. But the couple was still having a rough time. They were broke and they were worn out from their difficult trip. They wanted to marry and there were no priests available. The patron was not a man to give up easily and they believed he would locate them sooner or later. A far away ranch was the perfect place to hide. The young people had made it to the uncle, traveling on two of the patron's "borrowed" horses. When John heard the story, he told Smith about it.

Smith offered to send the horses back, give young Juan a job as cook, and provide him and his lady a place to live. The young man could have all of the kitchen help he wanted and he would be safe on the 0 Ranch.

Juan jumped at the opportunity. His English was not good so the uncle was hired to help in the kitchen and interpret for Juan. Another room was added to the main house for Juan's uncle.

# Zero Smith

The next day two cowhands put the two Mexican horses on the train. The animals were bound for a Texas border town where Smith knew the brands would be recognized. There would be no papers showing where they had come from.

The plus side of the Mexican equation was that Franco's nephew was very well trained in the duties of a cook in a very sophisticated house. In addition to being an excellent cook, the man was also a very good baker. Smith wired for a priest and sent travel expenses. He hoped a holy man arriving from back east would know nothing of the dilemma the couple were in and would simply marry Juan and Lolita.

This proved to be true. The priest arrived and he did marry them. He was amply rewarded and he left soon after on the first available train. The 0 Ranch had a cook, and a good one. Perhaps a great one.

Juan was one of those rare and special people who loved to see other people eat the things that he made. It was not enough to just make food. Juan loved to watch the pleasure on the faces of those who ate his prepared foods and his baked goods. The cowhands at the 0 Ranch had never eaten this well in their lives. Few people anywhere had, and Juan was very happy. After feeding them his first meal, the men literally picked Juan

# Zero Smith

up and carried him on their shoulders around the large dining table, to the joy of all. When they put him down, both he and his new bride Lolita, had tears in their eyes. He was also grateful to Smith for making it all possible. He had Lolita and he had hungry people to feed. He was in heaven. Zero proposed a toast to Juan and Lolita and he welcomed them to their new home on the 0 Ranch.

Another living area was added to the ranch house and the newlyweds moved from their temporary space when their own permanent, more comfortable, quarters were ready.

The 0 Ranch was becoming home to people who had never known a home. It was becoming a safe haven for people who had never known safety. Pride in the brand was growing. The 0 Brand was worth fighting for.

Zero Smith gave some serious thought to the consequences of his action regarding Juan and Lolita. This was a new land, with respect for the rights of an individual to choose where to live, who to marry, where to work. In this country, no one was owned. Those days were over with the abolition of slavery. Smith recalled his grandfather saying, "In for a dollar, in for a thousand." That slogan had helped to make the family rich. He would deal with the patron's shooter if and when he came. The ranch needed a cook.

# Zero Smith

Another expression of his grandfather proved well worth remembering: "If it's worth having, it's worth fighting for. Zero Smith had been fighting for years over nothing. Now that he was building a ranch, if it became necessary he would fight with more zeal than his enemies could ever imagine.

One day the patron's man arrived and asked to speak with Juan. He rode a beautiful horse and was very well dressed in the rich Mexican style. His gun was a nickel-plated Colt .44. He had a very bright smile and eyes like a cobra. Zero saw the man ride up to the ranch hitching rail. He got down without being asked, which was a breach of common western courtesy. Apparently the man was used to being feared.

Smith introduced himself and said that Juan worked for the 0 Ranch now.

"No Seniõr, Juan works for my patron, Don Artega, just like always, and Lolita is betrothed to his son, Paulo Artega."

"I'm sorry, Seniõr. You have made a long trip for nothing. Juan and Lolita were married by a Catholic priest one month ago, and I have the paper to prove it."

"I have my orders, Seniõr Smith."

"Your orders can get you killed."

The Mexican shooter went for his gun and died there in the yard under his horse.

As he closed his eyes for the last time,

## Zero Smith

he said respectfully, "You are very good, Seniõr Smith."

# CHAPTER THIRTEEN

One day Zero said to Old John, "Do you still have those two horses that you "found"?

"Yes, sir."

"Want to sell them?"

"Yes, sir. I sure do."

"Let's have a look at them after work."

Old John had a few acres and a comfortable shack, down among the cottonwood trees along the stream that ran through town.

When Smith arrived he found it to be a very pleasant place. They sat on chairs John had made that were placed in the shade under the big cottonwoods. It was a cool, dark sanctuary on this hot day. They were near the stream and they could hear the sound of the water as it trickled over the rocks in the stream bed. They could also hear the sound of rustling cottonwood leaves as the summer breezes passed by.

John called it his "cottonwood music."

The sound of the leaves rustling and the water falling over the rocks was beautiful and peaceful. He said, "I just sit here and

# Zero Smith

listen and listen and I say to myself that I'm free, I'm free. I got a paper that say so. Mr. Karen had it made legal and all."

"I own this place. I got a paper that say that, too. I got the cottonwood music and I got a job with Miss Laura. Who could want more than that?"

Then he smiled, big as life. Both men felt good. John brought out the whiskey and they both smiled.

They drank in silence for a few minutes, each man with his own thoughts.

"You have a very nice place here, John," commented Smith, and he meant it.

Smith bought the horses, the saddles and the rest of the gear that John had found on them, including a good looking pair of spurs. The spurs were silver plated, with big Mexican star rowels. Both men were pleased with the deal.

Then Smith asked, "Do you know any good cowhands that might be looking for work?"

"Yes, sir. I do. My boy Todd has been a cowboy all his life. He's getting too old for the trail now. He's maybe fifty, and he's riding the grub line most winters but he's strong and he's a good cowboy. He told me he would like to settle around here one day so to be near his pa, but I suspect that it's because he knows this valley got the mildest winter in the territory."

Zero noticed how Old John opened up on his own turf. Nothing like land to make a man feel secure.

"Can you get word to your son?"

"Oh yes, sir. I can do that all right. Todd be glad to come here."

Todd showed up ten days later with another man. They were just about the saltiest looking black cowboys that Zero Smith had ever seen.

After introductions, Smith learned the other man's name was Randy, and he was, in several ways. The name's double meaning always brought on a few smiles. They were a capable looking pair. These two had been to the mountain. Each man was large, but Todd was the more powerful of the two. Their gear was well worn but in good shape and they were riding good, powerful horses. They both wore guns, and each man had a rope and a whip on his saddle horn. They wore big Texas style bat-wing chaps and large brimmed, beat up, dark cow hats hauled down hard in front and back. Nothing showed but their eyes and a hard serious look on their faces.

Smith told them the terms, and they hired on to ride for the 0 Brand.

"We're small now but one day I hope this outfit will be one that you can be proud to ride for."

In the days that followed, Todd and Randy proved to be better than Smith could have hoped for. The men worked well individually and as a team. They had been partners a long time and they hired on together or they didn't hire on at all. Partners among cowboys was not uncommon and Smith was happy to have them.

He was sure they knew more about cows than he did, so instead of quitting the freight company, he made Todd foreman of the 0 Ranch and Randy was made the segundo. When Smith told them of his decision, Todd's face lit up with a big bright smile just like his father's, and Randy let out a Texas yell that could be heard clear across Wyoming.

Then Todd frowned and said, "Mr. Smith, you know some men aren't going to want to work for a black man."

"Then we don't want them on the place."

"Yes, sir."

"By the way, Todd. Your father tells me you're pretty handy with that six-shooter.

To which Todd replied, "I'm a black man and I'm still alive."

This time it was Smith's turn to put on a big smile. He could imagine some of the difficulty these two men must have had working the Texas outfits, and vowed that there would be none of that on this ranch.

# CHAPTER FOURTEEN

Zero Smith took a day off and rode up into the high country. There was a bench on the far west side of the ranch and from there it was all up hill until one came to the snow. He didn't go that far, but he did go far enough to see over most of his property.

The land was a dozen kinds of green with tan grass and blue sage in the dry areas and yellow and red leaves on the vine maples. There were meadows of blue wild flowers and others of lavender. Some meadows were pink with millions of little shooting stars.

Way off on a dry hillside he could see red Indian paint brush and all around were stands of shimmering aspen and dark pine. The entire scene was domed by an immense blue, cloudless sky. It was truly beautiful country.

He rode up here to think. After soaking up the beauty of the place and the superb view of the green valley from this high up, he climbed down from his horse, sat beneath a big pine and gave some serious thought to

121

# Zero Smith

the new Zero Smith.

He was feeling much better about himself. So much so that he was frequently smiling on the inside these days. He reasoned that for the first time in years he was actually doing things for people other than himself.

Zero Smith's arrival in Pinedale was the beginning of a new era for him. Meeting Laura and buying the ranch had helped him on his road to becoming human again. He was fond of the new Zero Smith but he also knew it was a little soon to go back to his original name, and much too soon to consider going back east to head up the family businesses.

The change in Smith started when he met Laura and went to work for the Karen Freight Company. He showed Old John how to make a buck on the outlaws' horses and then he saved the wagons from being robbed. His cows were earning money for Mary Hightower. He had saved the two boys from going to jail by first scaring the hell out of them, and then giving them jobs which by now they seemed to like. Equally important, he had put a ranch together and stocked it with good cattle and good men to watch over them. He helped Juan and Lolita out of their problem and into marriage.

In less than three months he went from

being a fast gun drifter to a solid member of the community. He'd found two women that he was fond of and one in particular really had his head spinning.

This altruism suddenly was very suspect. Zero Smith wasn't sure if he really knew himself. Two things he was sure of, however. He had certainly changed since those first years after the war, and he felt much better about himself. He was on a roll and he hoped to keep it that way. He was having fun, like Juan, by making other people happy. He made another mental note that he was going to take a very dim view of anyone who attempted to cloud up and rain horribles down on his personal world.

On a previous ride to look at some of his property, Smith found a line cabin. It was situated up high with its back to the trees and it overlooked a vast view of the ranch. When he first arrived, none of the grass had been disturbed by wild life. No one had been there in a long time. He'd sent men to clean up the place and make repairs where necessary. Then he sent the boys up with all of the necessary supplies to outfit the place, so he could live there comfortably.

Books and brandy, plenty of food, good whiskey and a hammock. He sent lots of gun stuff plus extra ammunition. Smith planned to practice shooting in order to stay gun

# Zero Smith

sharp. One day he rode up to the old cabin and moved in.

When he was settled, he went outside to put up his horse in the adjacent lean-to. He repaired the corral gate, an item his men had overlooked. He found the water in the well to be clear and cold. There was also a snow melt creek near the cabin and he could use that water if necessary. The small creek was probably why the well water was as fresh as it was. The creek water was cold, but warmed more each day, and he used it for bathing.

Smith spent several days there, reading and lazing around. Many hours were given over to looking at the natural world around him. He enjoyed the sounds of the wind in the trees, the birds' songs and his horse munching grass. He enjoyed the changing colors of the sky and the clouds as the sun traveled across the heavens. Smith needed this down time. He'd lived this way many times before coming to Pinedale, but then he was aware only of danger. Now he was becoming aware of the good things in life. Zero Smith was changing.

# CHAPTER FIFTEEN

When Smith returned to the ranch, he was told by Todd that four or five men in town had hoorahed Josh, apparently because he was a mute. The men taunted him and then punched him around in a circle, until he swung back. Josh was a big strong kid. He'd hit one of the men and knocked out some of his front teeth. The man drew a gun and shot Josh. Luckily the bullet just grazed his left side. It had plowed a furrow deep enough to place a finger in. The men laughed, leaving Josh lying on the floor of the saloon in a pool of blood. Josh was not wearing a gun.

One of the saloon girls helped to get him to the doctor, where he was patched up. He rode back to the ranch alone. As he rode into the yard in front of the bunk house, he passed out and fell from his horse. The fall had opened the wound again and the cook cauterized a small part of it while Josh was still out. Later Josh explained to his brother Ben, with their usual pantomime language and a few pencil notes, just what had hap-

125

# Zero Smith

pened. It was further learned that Josh, who was a nice looking lad, was seeing that particular saloon girl on occasion. The men had given the girl a bad time for having anything to do with a man who couldn't talk. Apparently she had refused the advances of one of the men, and then when Josh came in, she greeted him warmly. That was enough to start the ruckus.

Zero looked in on Josh and then went to town.

Todd said to the men who were present, "Did you see the look on his face? That man can be cold."

That was the first time any of Smith's crew had a glimpse of another side of their boss-man's character. One of the men even got a chill thinking about it.

Of course, none of his men knew anything about Smith's reputation with a gun. Neither did anyone in the valley except Laura, and she knew very little.

Smith didn't have much to go on, but he did know the name of the saloon girl. Her name was Dolly. She was a lively redhead who worked in the Stud Horse Saloon.

When Zero rode into town, he recognized two horses. They belonged to Todd and Randy, but he didn't see the two men anywhere. He entered the Stud Horse Saloon and asked for Dolly. The bartender pointed her out through the smoke and the noise. Smith walked over and offered to buy her a drink. They sat at a table and Smith explained that Josh worked for him, and that he wanted to know the whole story and who the men were that had given one of his cowhands a hard time.

"Those creeps are right over there." She nodded toward a table where four men were playing poker. She explained that this wasn't the first time that they had teased Josh, but it was the first time that they had done him any physical harm.

At first they had all punched him around in a circle, each one swinging at him in turn and the others taunting him to speak up. When Josh hit back, the man drew his gun and fired.

"Mr. Smith, you be careful of them, particularly the one in the black leather vest. He's real mean.

"I heard him say to one of his friends that Josh worked for a man who was a spy for the Yankees. Did they mean you, Mr. Smith?"

"Thank you, Miss Dolly. I appreciate the help you gave Josh. I'm right fond of that young man. Now it might be best if you left the room for a few minutes," Zero said, while tipping his hat to her.

"So am I fond of him, Mr. Smith," she said, leaving, though she stopped just around the corner to watch.

Smith stood up and walked slowly toward them. He approached so the man in the black leather vest would be directly opposite from where he stood. Softly, Smith said, "I understand that you clowns hoorahed one of my cowhands and he wasn't wearing a gun. Well, gentlemen, I'm wearing a gun. Try me."

The whole room was quiet. The leather vest man sneered and said, "You're that Yankee spy. I was hoping to meet up with you. I hear you're real fast."

The man got up slowly. As he did so, he pulled his gun and fired it into the floor. Smith had put a bullet between his eyes and blown out the back of his head. Smith shot the next three men so fast that it sounded like one bullet. One man tried to shoot Smith from his chair, and Smith shot him in the heart. The man to the left of Leather Vest was a cross draw, and when seated his hands were very close to his pistol grip. Smith just shot up both his hand and his pistol grip. The bullet ricocheted off the pistol and into the man's side, making an ugly wound that looked, ironically enough, very like the one Josh received, only much deeper. He was gut shot and was to die a slow agonizing death.

The fourth man was a knife thrower and very fast. He would have killed Smith but for the bullet in his throat. The knife went by with force, but the man's aim and his life were spoiled a split second before he threw.

Three men were dead in the blink of an eye and a forth man working on it. The man grimaced in pain and Smith noticed the man had some front teeth missing.

Those people in the room were sure they heard only two shots. Smith's gun was already holstered, and some weren't even sure he had done all of the shooting.

# Zero Smith

# CHAPTER SIXTEEN

Zero Smith walked out of the Stud Horse Saloon to a fame he didn't want. The town went crazy. No one was sorry to see the four men put under. Most of the townspeople would have preferred to have seen it done sooner. No one wept over these scoundrels. Smith usually felt a little diminished by the death of anyone, except during those years after the war, of course, when he felt nothing. There were witnesses so there was no trouble with the sheriff.

The four dead men were guilty of nearly everything and suspected of more. Yet here in Pinedale there were no warrants on any of them. Smith prodded the sheriff to send out feelers to other lawmen to see if there were rewards on any of them.

The sheriff was really confused. Bodies were showing up all over the place. His peace of mind was shattered and all of it caused by that near nitwit driver for the Karen Freight Company, who was collecting reward money left and right.

# Zero Smith

"Another lucky shot, Smith?" the sheriff asked, sarcastically. He was catching on.

In the past, after Smith was in a shootout, he just rode on and disappeared, but this time his life was to become much more complicated. He left town hurriedly, and was soon joined by Randy and Todd. He pulled his horse up to a walk beside them and said, "You heard?"

"Boss, we was there, on the upstairs balcony."

Randy added, "We thought you might need a little moral support."

Todd and Randy were both wearing big grins.

"I almost did. The knife was fast. It's dangerous to think only in terms of guns. The fat's in the fire now. Every one of those men probably has people who will want revenge. In addition to that, when the word gets out, every kid trying to make a name for himself will be gunning for me.

"Leather Vest seemed to think I was a Yankee spy. Either of you ever hear of anyone referring to me as a spy? I was in the war, but it was strictly Yankee Cavalry. I served with Galway's Raiders."

The two men shook their heads.

Todd allowed that he hadn't heard anything about spying, one way or the other.

"When we get back to the ranch, Todd, I

want you to call all of the men together. I'll talk to them. In the meantime, I'm going to pack a few things to go on a trip. I'm not really going to leave, but I want everyone to think I have. I'll be up at the line cabin where the boys took the supplies. It's up on that high bench yonder. Say nothing to nobody. Just that I've gone. If you need to come up, come cautious and use this whistle call." Smith then demonstrated his oscillating high-low whistle call.

Back at the ranch when the men were assembled, Smith addressed them.

"I'm going away for awhile. Todd here will be in charge while I'm gone. The bank will notify him when the cattle will be coming in. When you go to the cattle pens to receive our new critters, you go armed and with all hands, but quiet like. You don't start any trouble. Now get this, nobody goes anywhere alone. I don't want any of you to get mixed up in a shooting. When you go to town for supplies, go in groups of six or more. Then get back here as quickly as you can. If there is any gun work to be done, I'll come back and handle it.

"Your pay will be delivered to you by the bank's people on the first of every month. I'd feel a lot better knowing you were all safely hunkered down here at the ranch.

"If some of you get randy, just try to keep

the lid on it for a few days and we'll see if this blows over. The banker will notify Todd when cattle are arriving. They will mostly come by the railroad.

"Remember, when you men go to town or to the rail yards to pick up the cattle, I'm repeating, that it's imperative you go armed and in groups. Todd, six or seven men at a time, more if you like. Now get this, Nobody goes to town alone, or even in pairs.

"Naturally I can't order you to stay here, but I'd like it best if you all would just hang out until I come back. Todd, you better hire some more men. Get mature people if you can. It's quite possible that this whole thing will blow over in a few days, or more likely, in a couple of weeks. However long I'm gone, you'll get your pay. That's it for now. Be careful and good luck."

Smith turned to Todd and asked him to join him in his office.

The two men sat drinking whiskey and feeling its fire burn on its way down.

Smith began, "Todd there's more to this than meets the eye. The man in the black leather vest that I shot today is king-size trouble. I think he comes from a hill family that's been feuding for generations. Their name is Walters.

Leather Vest is a sometime assassin. The whole clan is long on guns and short on brains. They're really only trouble because there are a lot of them, not because they're any good. There are two cousins that can be bad actors, but the last I heard of them they were back in Tennessee.

"At any rate, I want you to stock up on ammo and food and fortify this place. Sand bag around the bunk house at least belt high. The same for the main house. Keep ten horses in the corral at all times, the best ones, and rotate them so they keep fit.

"Post guards and patrol the stream so that no one dams up our water supply. You better fill a few water barrels just in case. If you have to, you can always use the old well. Even though it doesn't taste very good, the water is all right. Can you think of any thing else, Todd?"

"No, but there is a man I would like to hire. He's likely to be expensive. He's the best tracker around these parts and he can shoot about as well as any man, except maybe yourself."

"You suit yourself about who you hire, Todd. We can afford it, whatever it costs. If you need something, you get it. We have plenty of money."

As they walked outside, Smith turned to Todd, and said, "By the way, Todd, I'd like to see you shoot. Do you see those two old buggy wheels sitting way over there? Try for the spokes."

It was a good distance away and would be a difficult shot for anyone that wasn't expert. Todd drew and fired from the hip. He blew away five wheel spokes. Like most savvy gunmen, Todd only carried five bullets in his six-shooter, so the hammer was always on an empty chamber. Both men had a big smile on their faces. Then Zero fired, and easily blew away five more spokes. Somehow the little game made the two men feel closer to each other. Neither said anything, but they both knew it.

Both men reloaded, and leaving Todd in charge, Smith headed for the line cabin.

# CHAPTER SEVENTEEN

The next morning Todd and Randy rode to the next town to send a telegram to Todd's tracker friend. His name was Cheyenne Williams, sometimes abbreviated to "Shy" though he was anything but that.

Cheyenne Williams was Indian, Hawaiian, Negro and white, of about equal amounts. He was handsome and he was trouble. He did most things to excess and loved doing them. He was all man and all rascal. If he knifed or shot up a jealous husband or a possessive boyfriend, he said it was 'icing on the cake.'

Todd knew Cheyenne was unpredictable, and if he was holed up with a woman he might not respond to the telegram. He was so cantankerous that he might not respond just on general principle. Usually money talked, but not always. Todd was smiling at Randy as he said, "If and when he gets this telegram, I sure hope he's broke. I hope he is not with a woman and I hope he's hungry."

As it happened, Cheyenne did get the

# Zero Smith

telegram. He didn't have a woman and he was broke. Dead broke. He also had the world's greatest hangover. The pounding in his head was like the world's biggest blacksmith pounding the world's biggest hammer on the world's biggest anvil. All of this was aggravated by a tapping on his boot by the world's smallest stationmaster who, though speaking in a soft respectful voice, seemed to be shouting at Williams in what to him, seemed to be a foreign language.

Through a barely opened eye, Cheyenne recognized his "Innkeeper," who was trying to tell him something. Cheyenne had been using the station as his temporary shelter, even though the nice little man had suggested that perhaps Mr. Cheyenne Williams might care to lodge elsewhere. The extraordinarily handsome plainsman sometimes had a fierce demeanor and most people were inclined to give him lots of room, including many a sheriff. Those that didn't soon learned that they'd made a serious mistake.

Williams reached out with a big paw and pushed the nice little man right out the door of his own station, and then locked him out.

"Mister, count your blessings," said one of the town loafers who was witness to the unkind treatment. "You're lucky to be alive. When Cheyenne has a hangover, he's the meanest thing that walks."

Later that same afternoon when Cheyenne finally gathered himself all the way up into a full slouched position, the stationmaster assumed that Mr. Williams was ready to hear what he had to say.

Wrong.

Cheyenne Williams simply turned over and went back to sleep. The stationmaster concluded the task was hopeless and, with his dignity feathers only slightly ruffled, gave up.

Four hours later when Cheyenne was nearly coherent, on his feet and in a thoroughly nasty mood, the nice little man, taking his life in his hands, delivered the telegram.

"You read it."

Cheyenne's breath nearly bowled over the little fellow.

"You've been offered a job and they sent money for your fare if you choose to go. The train that goes near Pinedale stops at Rockford. That's about fifteen miles from Pinedale. The train will be through here tomorrow morning about sunup."

"What I need is a drink. A little hair of the dog."

"They sent money for that, too."

Suddenly the little man had Cheyenne William's undivided attention.

Cheyenne sat up straight and grabbed

# Zero Smith

the little man by the front of his jacket and said, "Say that again."

He did.

"Who sent money and they want me to go where?"

The stationmaster explained it all again, and then was suddenly dragged and half carried by Cheyenne, who held the little man by the coat collar, to the bank to get the money order cashed. Cheyenne Williams grabbed the money from the bank clerk without counting it and headed straight for the saloon where he bought a bottle. He pulled the cork with his teeth and spit it onto the floor, took a big pull of the whiskey that shook him all over and a few minutes later was wearing a big smile. He checked over the ladies present and reasoned that, after all, there weren't any trains due till morning. There was time enough to take on "supplies."

# CHAPTER EIGHTEEN

Early the next morning, Cheyenne Williams took what money he had left and two bottles of whiskey from a store whose window he'd smashed, and boarded the train, much to the relief of the station- master and the regret of a redhead with great legs. The little man got his dignity and his office back, but it would be weeks before he regained his composure and once again saw himself as a major link in modern western transportation.

The redhead got a chance to rest, but unlike the stationmaster, it was only a matter of hours before she made a major contribution to modern western socialization.

Cheyenne plopped into the nearest seat just as the train pulled out. He felt like death. If it came he would have embraced it with the same eagerness that he would have embraced a woman.

At the moment he was attempting to achieve the impossible. He was attempting to find a comfortable position for his hungover body on the hard bucking seat of the passenger car, which at the moment seemed to him, second only to the ride on a green bronc.

He had already conceded to the smoke and cinders that floated around in the car. It was to be another dark and dismal day for Cheyenne Williams, even though it was bright and sunny outside. He still had the world's biggest blacksmith pounding with the world's biggest hammer on the world's biggest anvil inside the world's most aching head.

When he boarded the train, Williams found himself sitting across from two Texas cowhands who were raised on cows and racism. They watched with distaste as Cheyenne slouched near them in the car. One of them said, "I'm not riding in the same car with no Indian or mixed blood or whatever he is!"

Cheyenne fixed that so fast the cowhand never knew what happened. Cheyenne actually picked the man up and launched him right out through the window of the moving train. Glass flew every which way. He then put his huge knife to the throat of the other cowhand, disarmed him and whispered, "Now it's your turn. You're getting off. You go through that window or you will wear this blade in your guts for the rest of your life, which would be in about ten seconds."

"Yes, sir." And out he went.

Cheyenne expertly twirled the man's .38 caliber revolver a couple of times and then fired off two shots at two different wooden buttons in the ceiling of the railroad car. He was immediately sorry. The gun explosions shattered the wooden buttons, but they also shattered, so it seemed, his head, his spine and all the rest of his nerve endings. He decided the gun wasn't much good and tossed it to a ten-year-old boy who was a bug-eyed witness to these proceedings. Cheyenne mumbled something about it being a kid's gun.

Several people moved away from the broken window, but nobody said a word. Some were too scared to move and sat miserably in the draft and smoke that came through the open window.

Cheyenne walked to the other end of the car and selected a new seat. He stared at the man occupying it until the man got up and moved quickly away.

It had been said of Cheyenne Williams that if he was in one of his nasty moods, even a grizzly bear would move out of his way.

He then eased into a slouch against the chair back, pulled his hat down over his eyes and went into his half-sleep. It allowed him to rest but still be on his guard, a habit he learned early in life.

# Zero Smith

Like other wild things, his was a world of predation, and he had acquired the tricks and tools of survival early. By now, these, like his knives, were honed to a razor sharp edge.

One unhappy citizen complained to the conductor about the deplorable behavior of that dreadful person shooting pistols and throwing those people out of windows and off the train and demanding to know what he was going to do about it.

The conductor's mamma didn't raise any foolish children. His answer was to ignore her as though she were invisible, leave the lady standing there, and to find very important work to do in another part of the train.

The remainder of the trip to Pinedale was uneventful. Cheyenne drank and slept most of the way. When Cheyenne arrived in Pinedale, he was met by Todd and Randy. They saw a plainsman in buckskin who had a handsome, lined face and a young, powerful body. He was lean except in the shoulders, which looked to be overly powerful. He had long, dark, wavy hair that was tied with a band around his forehead and again in clumps on each side of his handsome face. The clumps of hair were tied with the homemade red wool of some far away tribe in the southwest.

He had the straight nose of whites,

slightly thicker lips of the Hawaiian and Negro and bright white teeth. When he smiled, his entire face lighted up. He had coffee colored skin and mostly the look of an Indian. His ruggedly handsome face was a composite of the best of all four races. His black hat was flat crowned with a wide brim and when worn low over his eyes, gave him a foreboding look. The hat also added to his height, and he was already taller than most men.

He was something special to look at. No one was sure why exactly, but if one thought about it long enough, the reason was his eyes. They were gray with flecks of yellow-amber and very wolflike. There was a wildness to his eyes when he was calm, and when he was angered, he looked positively crazed. When he was like that, few people could look him in the eye.

He had a short fuse and was vicious when fighting, yet he could charm people right out of their socks. This was particularly true of women. Wherever Cheyenne Williams went, there were usually several "barefooted" women. Besides having a wonderful smile, he was articulate. He romanced women the way Cyrano de Bergerac might have done, but in a slightly less sophisticated way and he had similar trouble with husbands and outraged swains, who frequently demanded satisfaction.

These fellows said dumb and corny things like, "Pistols at dawn." Cheyenne Williams, who tended to overreact, just beat the hell out of them, right there on the spot.

By the time the swelling left their blackened eyes, their broken noses, and their broken fingers mended, usually all ten of them, Cheyenne Williams was long gone. None of these insulted fellows would ever hold pistols again, but they would be more apt to live longer and more useful lives.

Many others had not. If they'd made a bad call and let pride interfere with their judgment, they were dead. Some were buried, but some were just left for the vultures.

On a darker day, Williams might just as easily have snapped their spines or given them a high voice, or both, and perhaps still killed them.

Cheyenne led the two men straight to the saloon with just about the same speed that a rented horse returns to its home stable.

"He's a tracker all right," said Randy." He found the saloon without even opening his eyes."

Todd answered, "It's a good thing. If he opened both of his eyes at the same time, he might bleed to death."

Williams' eyes were very bloodshot.

Todd could see the man was in tough

shape and he sympathized, having been there a time or two himself.

They'd walked to the hotel saloon from the depot. Cheyenne carried his saddle as though it was weightless, not on his shoulder like most cowhands would, but held by the saddle horn, out at his side.

Todd observed that while the man may have a terrible pounding head, there was certainly nothing wrong with his strength.

Cheyenne was alert enough to notice the boys were leading an extra horse and a very good one at that. A big sorrel stallion with a blaze, four white stockings and wearing an 0 Brand. Cheyenne liked the horse right away but said nothing.

When the three men walked into the saloon, it suddenly got quiet. They could feel the tension in the room. They saw more Texas cowboys. They wore the usual Texas signs which were big wide brim hats, floppy bat wing chaps and Mexican, big rowel spurs, and they were all wearing guns.

Cheyenne ordered whiskey. Todd and Randy ordered whiskey and food from the bartender.

Nothing came of the tension in the room. For one thing, the cowboys were mostly that, just boys, and Todd and his two friends were just about the saltiest looking men that these young Texans had ever seen. Especially so was the mixed blood Indian, who was armed as they were with a six gun, but also with a huge, wicked looking knife.

Cheyenne felt better after several drinks, but he made it plain that he wasn't ready for anything so daring as food. He did try some coffee while the boys had dinner. It allowed them to catch up on old times.

"So it was you two that sent me the money. I wasn't sure who did. The little stationmaster seemed to be afraid to get close to me when he was reading the telegram, so I only heard parts of it. Mostly, I heard there was traveling expenses, which as you might have guessed, with this Cheyenne translates into whiskey.

"Contrary to what you might think I'm actually tapering off. Just some hair of the dog."

They continued to talk of old times as they ate. Todd suggested that Cheyenne might share some of the food.

Cheyenne replied that he didn't feel hungry just yet. Perhaps in a day or two. The 0 Ranch men minded their own business, ignoring the dirty looks they received from the Texans, finished their meal, and left.

Cheyenne's eyes looked so bad that Todd was sure the man didn't know who had met him at the train until after he'd had his third drink.

Williams didn't binge like this often or he would not have lived this long. He had too many enemies in all four camps. He'd lived with them all. The Indian, the Black, the Hawaiian and the white.

Cheyenne Williams had the unique gift of sliding in and out of each culture with the ease of a chameleon. The Souix and Blackfeet knew him to be a great warrior. They called him "Wims." He had gone on horse stealing raids with braves from each tribe. Always against their enemies such as the Crow or the Ute and even against the Shoshone. On these occasions "Wims" had counted many coups and taken many scalps.

The three men spent the night at a safe camp with a low fire, well back in thick timber. The hobbled horses were their watch dogs. When the horses ears came up so would the three trail-wise men, guns in hand.

They talked of outfits they had all ridden for, of long gone fights, fun and women. They talked of times that brought mixed emotions to the group. Everything from loud laughter to sorrow and an occasional solemn quiet for a lost friend. Memories and emotions came forward that might never have surfaced had each man been alone, but together they found a strength in each other, and even a willingness to open up and talk. The aid of a little booze didn't hurt.

# Zero Smith

# CHAPTER NINETEEN

Todd knew "Shy" was always armed to the teeth, and even when he was drunk his guns were clean and cared for. His elk leather gunbelt was both light in color and in weight. The holster was his own special design and carried a walnut grip Colt .44 below his right hand. If he thought it necessary, Cheyenne, who could shoot with either hand, had a second Colt and holster that he clipped on the gun belt below his left hand. Both holsters were tied down to his legs, and there was a sixteen inch long knife sheathed just to the left of his unusual belt buckle. The buckle was a foot wide and made of polished moose antler. Hidden behind the belt buckle was a double barrel .44 Derringer. In addition, he carried two Colt .44's as saddle guns, plus a Winchester.

He wore high Apache style boot-moccasins that carried a lesser blade in each. When he was serious, he also wore a knife in a sling hung from around his neck and down his back under his buckskin shirt. He called it

# Zero Smith

"being prepared."

Todd exclaimed, "Prepared, Hell! You're more like a walking arsenal."

Cheyenne could stick a playing card at forty feet with any of his knives and with either hand, though not many had seen this display of skill and lived to tell about it. An exception was his Cheyenne Indian grandfather, who had taught him knife throwing.

This grandfather had learned his throwing skills from a white French trapper. Knife throwing was important partly because guns often misfired. This was especially true in earlier days. But knives were as reliable as one's skill. That simple philosophy had saved the life of Cheyenne Williams on more than one occasion. Another reason for relying on the knife was that it was a silent killer. A bow and arrows were silent, but during wet weather a bow was not likely to shoot reliably if the rawhide thong got wet. For this reason, Indians were sometimes reluctant to do battle or go raiding during wet weather. At any rate, under his grandfather's tutelage, young Cheyenne Williams mastered the several arts of knife throwing by the time he was fourteen years old. This was a rare skill among Indians probably because good knives were hard to come by and the risk of losing the thrown knife was great.

His six shooter skills came later, and

with diligent practice he mastered handguns as well as the knife by the time he turned seventeen.

It was begrudgingly said about Williams on occasion that he was certainly no ordinary man.

There were many women who would concur with great enthusiasm.

The men didn't know quite what that dubious compliment meant, but most agreed that it was true in the positive sense. Whereas the women, judging by a different standard, knew exactly what the statement meant. Some of them just smiled smugly, and others wore a glazed eye as they looked back into their memory bank. Still others, who were not part of the chosen few, were merely envious.

As a tracker, Cheyenne Williams' great skill bordered on being mystical. The Indians claimed he could track even in the wide rivers and over solid rock, which was sometimes true. They thought the spirits helped him. This was also true on occasion. Credit was sometimes due to the spirits right enough. Both kinds.

The next morning when the three men rode into town, there was a reception committee in the middle of the street waiting for them. The two cowboys Cheyenne threw off the train had somehow found horses and must have ridden all night to get here. Bruised and scratched, the two men, now backed by several of their friends, were a lot braver than they were the day before. These Texans were a mixed bag ranging in age from sixteen to forty-five. There were eight armed men, two carrying rifles. One of the older men in the group had a rope with a hanging noose already tied, which left little doubt as to their intentions.

Todd's group had all been there before at one time or another. The feeling brought goose bumps to Todd's arms. He figured that he couldn't have found two better men in the entire west to side with him just now.

It was showdown time and he suggested that the three of them "Just stomp the hell out of these Texicans."

Cheyenne held his hand up to stay Todd and Randy. He then walked his fancy new stallion the hundred feet up to the group of cowboys.

"First, I came to make medicine. You boys don't want all of this trouble. I hear this country needs cowhands. Second, I'll kill the first one of you that moves."

The one with the hangman's noose thought he was a faster draw. He pulled his six-gun and shot off his own knee cap.

From twenty feet away, Cheyenne had put his big long knife in the cowboy's throat the second he drew. As the man wearing the knife toppled from his horse, a second cowhand went for his gun and Cheyenne shot him through the heart. A third received a knife through his hand the moment he touched his gun, and the salt dissolved right out of the rest of those boys. Two of the men vomited and the rest of the Texicans were stunned.

This Indian in front of them had more bark on him than any man they had ever seen. If he would have said "jump," they would have answered, "Yes, sir. How high and how far?"

In another minute they might all have been dead because Todd and Randy were coming at a run with guns cleared.

Without looking back, Cheyenne raised his hand to stay Todd and Randy, who pulled their mounts to a sliding halt.

They saw the man with the noose wearing a knife in his throat and very dead, another dead man sprawled under two nervous horses, and the surviving men slowly shucking their handguns with fingertips only. One man was shucking his iron with his left hand because his right hand still had a knife stuck in it. Cheyenne wasn't holding anything but his saddle horn.

Todd and Randy were both smiling when Randy said, "The brother is powerful persuasive." And he was. Powerful.

The rest of the cowhands, six in number and all Texicans, were now wearing their docile hats and apparently did not miss the men that had been killed by Cheyenne. Both dead men were still lying in the street where they might be for some time. They were not liked by the other Texicans, the town didn't have a sheriff, and the barber undertaker didn't work for free.

Cheyenne rode up to the man with a knife through his hand and said, "Look over there."

When the man turned his head, Williams quickly pulled the knife free. The cowhand fainted and started to fall from his horse. Cheyenne held him up and, eyeing the other Texicans, calmly wiped the blood from his knife on the cowhand's sleeve and then honed the ten inch blade on the man's leather chaps. No one moved, and the Texicans were stunned.

Cheyenne Williams looked the group over and picked the oldest man.

"You, climb down and get my big knife."

The cowhand attempted to pull the knife from the dead man's throat and the corpse made strange sounds. The cowhand fell to his knees and vomited.

Cheyenne looked at Todd and Randy and said, "Watch them."

Cheyenne dismounted, walked over to the dead man, put his moccasined foot against the dead man's face and pulled the knife out. There was a horrible sucking sound as it came out and several of the Texicans turned green. Cheyenne calmly wiped the knife clean on the dead man's shirt. He looked each man in the eye, and said, "You boys stick to cattle, because guns can get you killed."

When Cheyenne had mounted up, and things were starting to return to normal, Todd asked, "What are you boys doing so far from home?"

"We come all the way from Texas," said one fellow.

"We've just delivered a herd of cattle to the corrals. They belong to a Mr. Z. Smith."

One of them smiled and said, "After we've seen the elephant, we'll be looking for work. Except Boyd there. He's hankering to go on to Montana."

Todd spoke up, "Have you boys got your pay yet?"

"Just enough to howl with. The rest is to come from Mr. Smith's agent," answered one of the men.

"Well, boys. There's been some kind of a mix-up here. I'm the foreman for Mr. Smith and those cattle were supposed to be delivered to Pinedale. That's eighteen miles from here, and the Pinedale banker has the money. How about you fellows giving a hand with the stock as far as Pinedale and I'll see if I can get you a little bonus money. We'll all stay the night and leave in the morning. What do you say?"

"We should get a bonus for getting that herd together. Some of them were so rank we were lucky to gather them at all."

"How do we know you are the foreman for Mr. Smith?" from one.

"Seems doubtful, you being a black man and all," from another.

"You don't, but I'm the only one authorized to receive that herd, so without me you won't get your money and besides you're not there yet. Those cows go to Pinedale."

"We've never worked for a black man before."

Cheyenne Williams glared at the talker, who was really only a lad, and the boy added, "Sir."

"You won't be working for me. You'll be working for Mr. Zero Smith."

There was a silence.

"Did you say, Zero Smith?"

"The famous Zero Smith?"

"The gunfighter?"

"I'd sure like to meet that man."

"So would I."

Todd and Randy smiled.

The man's name was like honey to a bear cub.

"Does the famous Zero Smith really own all of these cattle?"

Even Cheyenne was surprised.

"Todd, if he is as good as they say, why does he want me?"

"He doesn't. I do."

Todd continued, "Smith said that I could hire anyone I wanted. I been working with Randy so long I figured it was about time I classed up my act." Cheyenne saw the twinkle in Todd's eye as he said it. As usual, even Randy had a big wide smile.

"But why me?" Williams persisted.

"Randy and me thought that it was time we helped you see the light and turned you from your sinful ways.

Randy piped up and said, "It's more like we was wanting to take sinning lessons from a pro."

Todd said with a big grin, "We'll get to those lessons later. Right now we have cattle to count and move. How many head in that herd?"

One of the Texans, who looked like a six foot wire, drawled, "About a thousand."

"We lost a few on the way." This from the boyish faced cowboy.

"Where did you boys start this herd?" Randy inquired.

# Zero Smith

"Mostly from the Red River country, but some came from way south of there."

Todd said, "If you Texans are at the corrals at sun up, you got a job."

Todd had given the Texans a chance to think it over and ride on out if they were of a mind to, with no hard feelings, after they delivered the cattle to Pinedale, of course.

He then rode to a different camp outside of town, accompanied by the other two men.

The Texans headed straight for the dance hall girls to "find the elephant," and they did.

# CHAPTER TWENTY

At sun up the next morning, the Texican were more than a little bent. Some of them were downright cork-screwed, but they all showed up.

All except the one who was going to Montana decided to stay.

The others said good-bye to the fellow with comments like, "Try to keep your hair."

"Watch out for Blackfeet,"

"Watch your back trail now and again."

"Stay sharp on this ride."

And the young man headed out for Montana. A perilous ride to be sure.

Todd told the boys of the possibility of a war with the Walters' clan, and suggested, "Boys, you better think hard on this one."

Todd gave the Texicans time to think it over and ride on if they chose to.

The Texas cowboys stayed. After all, there were wars back home too, and just to get there was risky. Back home, money was scarce and there were very few jobs.

In some cases just to ride across another

# Zero Smith

man's range was to put yourself at risk. You were either for a brand or against it, which meant you had to fight for it sometimes. If you chose to ignore both sides and ride on through, that too might require a fight. Sometimes you had to fight to avoid fighting. The logic was elusive, but there it was.

The Texans figured they would try this new work for awhile. There was trouble with most jobs and there was certainly trouble just getting back to Texas. If there was going to be gun trouble, then they wanted to side with the famous Zero Smith.

Todd gave the men a paper and they signed their names or made their mark. They were now riding for the 0 Brand.

One of the boys explained to Todd that the herd leader was a certain sorry-looking brindle steer and that if they just opened the gate and headed him in the right direction, the rest of the herd would follow.

Todd could see that the critter was all horn and hide and battle scared but knew full well that he was worth his weight in gold to any trail boss. After all, the steer had led an entire herd well over a thousand miles. Todd wanted that ugly steer to lead them the rest of the way to Pinedale while he still had the hang of it and the others would follow. Given another week in the stock pens and the cattle would probably forget who the leader was, and it would be like starting the entire herd all over again.

The next morning before dawn, Todd asked Cheyenne to see if the stockyard attendant was available. Cheyenne, who often had a unique sense of humor, charged into the attendant's quarters and literally lifted the man out of bed.

He put the man's hat on his head, hauled, pushed and half carried the terrified fellow outside. Then he stood him up in front of Todd, Randy and the rest of the crew, still in his long johns, with his bare feet in a fresh cow pie. The 0 Brand people just broke up laughing.

The fellow was more than a little upset by his treatment at the hands of the 0 outfit and grumbled something about these people taking his cows before he got paid his lot fee.

Cheyenne gave him a killing look and asked if he was implying that those honest cowhands didn't ride for the brand.

The attendant backed down quickly and said, "Oh, no, sir! I'd be the last person to imply any such thing."

Todd and Randy smiled over that one, as these cattle were wearing every brand in Texas except the right one. Not a one of them had yet been branded with the 0 Brand.

That historical day, the Zero Smith outfit moved one thousand and forty-three head

# Zero Smith

safely to the Smith range near Pinedale, Wyoming Territory. The Texans did get a small bonus.

Wyoming Territory, where the Smith ranch was located, was a far ride from Texas, but in many ways the two areas were much the same. The people cared about cows and the cows cared about grass and they all cared about water which flowed in abundance from the snowcapped peaks. They also cared about survival in rough country because this was very rough country. It was tough on both the people and the critters. If they weren't tough, they didn't last. The Wyoming Territory was an area of extremes. It was dry and arid, and lush and green. It was very hot in summer and cold in winter. Occasionally it was so cold that cattle, if they were caught in the open by an icy wind, were known to freeze solid standing up. At certain times of the year there were violent thunder storms. Lightning could strike a large pine tree and cause it to explode, sending very large, deadly chunks of the tree sailing through the air to maim or kill both horse and rider. The temperatures were extreme seasonally and often within one day. A rider could put on and take off much of his clothing several times in one day.

Westerners had a saying out here: "If you don't like the weather, wait five minutes."

# Zero Smith

From Texas to Wyoming, the country was one of extremes—hot summers and bitter cold winters. This part of the west was noted for violent thunderstorms which often caused flash floods, grass fires and land slides. Indians, too, were a problem. They didn't much cotton to the idea of the white eyes taking their land and slaughtering their buffalo for hides. Who could blame them. On the plus side there were vast open grasslands, thick forests and for the most part, plenty of water.

The country had a big sky and marvelous panoramas of mountains, valleys, magnificent undulating lands and all of it good for cattle. The buffalo had prospered here without any help from man. Cattle would, too. And they did.

It was still the most beautiful country that Zero Smith had ever seen. He was enthralled with the beauty of the place. He loved the snowcapped mountains and pine forests that went on forever, grass to the horizon and water nearly everywhere, all domed by an immense blue sky. Wherever Smith looked, the vistas were majestic. He'd planted his feet here, and here he was going to stay.

The long arduous trail drive had taken much of the salt out of even the wildest cattle.

Todd reasoned the time to brand them

was when they were still trail weary. He even figured a way to do it without exposing the crew to the guns of rawhiders, rustlers, herd cutters or the Walters' clan.

They built log barricades and branded behind them. He also had two outriders patrolling just beyond rifle range from the branding area.

At Smith's suggestion, Todd sent a rider into town to get any news that Old John may have heard regarding the Walters' clan. He didn't want to be surprised by any of that bunch.

He informed the new ranch hands how Smith had faced three men in a gunfight in the Stud Horse Saloon when Josh was hoorahed by the town toughs. It was unfortunate that one of the men killed had so many nasty relatives. However, Zero Smith was determined to plant the rest of the family if they came here looking for trouble.

The new herd mixed in with the previously acquired cattle. The Texas boys settled into a ranch and a life style that they could be proud of. The food was good and each man was treated with the respect he'd earned by bringing the herd a thousand miles up the trail.

Here there was work. Here the Texicans had good jobs, good horses and better food than any cowhand had a right to expect. They had money in their pockets and none of them would have to ride the grub line come winter. Back home, Texas had not yet recovered from the war, and between the carpetbaggers and the outlaws, it was root hog or die.

In Texas at that time there were few jobs and very little money. Because there was no market, the price of beef had fallen to the point where some ranchers didn't even bother to run their fall gather. Many of the cattle turned wild. Some of those wild cows had not seen a rider in five or six years. Many had seven foot horns, and those from the East Texas breaks, or wooded areas, often carried a pound of two of moss on their horns.

The long drive to Wyoming had settled down even the wildest critters to a point where by using enough ropes, even the rankest were branded. These wilder critters usually required several more ropes than the others. Sometimes as many as five ropers were all taking a dally at the same time and all pulling in different directions, just to immobilize the critter long enough to get a brand on his hide. Then it was tricky work to get the ropes off. Some of those big, rank longhorns wore a rope or two until the ropes rotted off. The boys went through ropes, but the job proceeded. They were intent upon putting the 0 Brand on all of Smith's cattle as fast as possible.

# Zero Smith

With pine knot fires and the big 0 branding irons glowing red hot, the branding continued inside the barricades, which held the cattle in closer than if they had done the job on the open range.

Two mounted cowboys worked as header and healer and three mounted riders helped on the wildest critters. Another two riders worked as the gatherers. Three men worked the hot irons and kept the fires burning bright. It was hot and dusty work. The air was rank with the smell of burned hair and hide. The calves were wrestled to the ground and branded where they fell. Gradually the range was beginning to be dotted with cattle wearing the 0 Brand. The horn work was to be left for another time unless it was critical.

There were several serious problems as they were herded first to the branding fires. Of the many, four cases were the worst. The first was a steer with a horn that was growing right around and back into his left eye. The critter was in pain and already blind in that eye. He was shot, butchered and eaten, in that order.

A big Hereford cow had broken her right horn defending her calf against wolves, and some of the wolf still hung in putrid strips from that horn. Her calf was small, but seemed to be doing well enough. The men simply cleaned the bloody horn and painted it with axle grease and tar to keep the flies away. In time the cow got better.

The third was a "muley" with no horns but with a serious raw wound on the boss area, greatly aggravated by birds who were enjoying the feast of blood and maggots. This one was tarred, greased, and penned for observation.

The last was an old cow with splayed feet and cancer eye. Already blind in one eye and with impaired vision in the other, she was roped, led, and dragged off to be shot. However, before the shot was fired, three Cheyenne braves who were part of a hunting party rode toward camp. They saw Cheyenne Williams and howled a greeting to their old pal and sidekick, "Wims."

Cheyenne Williams saw the Cheyenne braves and rode out to meet them, howling his own greeting. The Indians palavered for awhile and Williams gave them the old cow. One brave was suspicious of the diseased looking cancer eye, and well he might be, but Cheyenne Williams said that he personally would eat from the cow with them now or at their lodges. He explained that only the eye was infected, but the red meat was perfectly good to eat. The cow was shot and dressed out. One of the braves was leading an extra horse and that critter was so loaded down with good beef from the freshly butchered cow that he half staggered all the way to the Cheyenne camp. When the horse arrived he fell down and refused to move until some of the beef was unloaded.

Cheyenne was invited to be their dinner guest in two days. He went. So did Randy and Todd. There was much ceremony. They smoked the pipe and offered to the four directions and the Earth and Sky. They ate, and the Indians were again much impressed by the knowledge of their brother who sometimes lived with the "white eyes," and who they called "Wims."

There was much joking about what a great dinner guest Cheyenne was because he brought the beef and the whiskey. They said with a laugh, "Wims, you and his friends can come to dinner at our lodges anytime so long as you bring whiskey and meat."

# CHAPTER TWENTY–ONE

Cheyenne told his Indian friends that he was now working for the 0 Ranch and he drew a diagram of the 0 Brand in the sand. He told them he was responsible for any cow with that brand. He also explained that the cows were not all marked yet with the 0 Brand but that they would be shortly, and that they needed help. If any of them wanted to help herd cows, the ranch would trade knives or hatchets for their help.

Laughing, they shook their heads. There were no takers. Warriors did not herd cattle.

Cheyenne said, "I am a warrior and I herd cattle sometimes."

They were shocked. They had witnessed this man in battle and knew him to be a great fighter. They would think on it. Todd, who was listening to all of this, gave a nod of approval. They could use the help but didn't expect anything to come of their offer.

The next day, the remainder of the hunting party went on, except for five young braves who agreed to stay for the branding

# Zero Smith

in exchange for each man receiving a good hunting knife. The young bucks thought the idea of branding a cow was ludicrous. No one ever marked the buffalo. They were just there to take as needed. They assumed it was the same with cattle.

"Wims" tried to explain to the young bucks that white men gained status by owning many cattle the way an Indian brave received status by having many horses. They laughed again because anyone knew a cow was just to eat but a horse could carry one into battle. They had always thought the white man was crazy, but now they were more convinced than ever.

Nonetheless, they still agreed to help gather cows for the branding in exchange for each man receiving knives.

Cheyenne showed them how to cut out several head from the main herd and to drive them into the branding corrals. This left the cowhands free to do the branding and the whole thing went faster. Before the work started, Cheyenne talked to both groups of men, the whites and the Indians, and warned them that he didn't want any squabbles of any kind between the whites and Indians or between whites and whites or Indians and Indians. If there were, they would have to deal with him.

The work continued to go well on both

sides. The white cowboys could use the help which made their job easier and the Indians could certainly use the knives and they actually had the easiest jobs. Cutting out cattle was tough on the horses but fairly easy on the riders.

The braves found their horses were getting tired as the day wore on so they were loaned additional ranch horses. They luxuriated in all of this horse flesh and they thought the work easy for such good knives. They laughed among themselves and agreed the white man was a fool.

Five days later, when the Indians received their knives, they were not so sure. Five days of gathering cows is just about four days and eight hours after the fun stops. It had become work and only their pride kept the young braves on the job. Todd threw in a blanket for each man. When the Indian braves left, they were happy with their new possessions. The knives were identical, and good ones, so there was no squabbling. They waved good-bye and rode off.

The branding wasn't finished but the crew would continue with that task for some time. It was to take longer than they thought.

# Zero Smith

# CHAPTER TWENTY–TWO

While Smith was up in the hills, Todd arranged to get the ranch supplies delivered by the Karen Freight Company. The town news came with the supply wagon driven by Todd's father.

Old John had seen some of the Walters' crowd in town and they looked to be a tough bunch, and more were expected. They seemed to be waiting for someone special because they met the stage on its daily arrival.

These low-lifes had already insulted several women in town, smashed windows, broken a few heads, and they had just arrived.

They told the locals that they were going to kill Zero Smith and destroy everything he owned. His woman, his cows, his cowhands, his dogs and his cat and anyone that helped him in any way. Because of this very real threat, Old John quickly dropped off the last of the supplies the 0 Ranch had requested and high-tailed out of there to make his other deliveries.

# Zero Smith

Unfortunately it didn't help Old John to hurry away from the ranch. He was seen by a Walters' gang member who was assigned to watch the ranch. The rider, instead of reporting back to town, decided to deal with this apparently helpless old man on his own. He cantered up to the wagon and told Old John, "Hold up there."

Old John had been well warned by Todd to shoot first, and he did just that.

He blew the rider right out of the saddle with a .12 gauge shotgun. He then reloaded his shotgun and drove back to the ranch to report the event to his son.

Todd gave Old John some whiskey to settle his nerves. A .12 gauge shotgun always required more nerve settling than a .44. Todd then asked his father to stay on at the ranch for a few days and sent Randy up to the line cabin to find Smith. Knowing that this was a very ticklish business, he cautioned Randy, "Go Injun sly."

When Randy arrived at the line cabin, Smith had been watching his approach for some time. Randy told of the incident with Todd's father. Smith decided it was time to go back to the ranch.

John was wondering how Miss Laura was going to get along with neither a team nor drivers. Smith promised to take care of it somehow, though he wasn't sure how just yet.

He considered bringing Laura out to the ranch for the time being, until the trouble was over, but knew she would put up a howl. He knew as long as she was in town she was in danger because of him. Her staying would make him vulnerable, too. It was not a good situation.

Laura must leave Pinedale. She had an Aunt Katherine who lived on a ranch a few day's coach ride from Pinedale. Zero slipped into town late one night and convinced Laura that she must close down the company and leave Pinedale, for her safety as well as his.

That same night they Injun'd out of town without being seen and made a cold camp by a stream. It was a nice moment for them away from the problems of the real world. There was a bright full moon and a soft, warm summer breeze. For a few hours it seemed as though they were the only people in the entire world.

The next day they stopped the stagecoach about a mile out of town. Laura got aboard and was off to Aunt Katherine's until Zero could get word to her that it was all over and safe for her to return.

The 0 Ranch was rapidly becoming a fortified compound. Todd had the hands working day and night building barricades and earth work defense structures for the perimeter of the house. There was even a barricade made to protect the horses.

The inside walls of the barn were stacked high with sand bags and bales of hay to protect the horses from stray or intentional bullets. If an attack came, the few horses could quickly be run inside the barn where they would be reasonably safe. What's more the barn could be easily defended by a few riflemen since they had an unobstructed field of fire.

Todd and the men had covered most of the angles to make the 0 Ranch impregnable.

Zero Smith had some ideas of his own along that line. He was giving thought to a "killing field" which would spell trouble for the Walters' clan if they rode out to the 0 Ranch.

# CHAPTER TWENTY–THREE

A few days later, Zero Smith was seated against a tree in the high country gazing out over the broad valley. He noticed a big herd of elk a little way off. Further down the canyon he could see some of his cattle, with some deer feeding near them.

Smith was taking stock of his present and his future. He was reasonably sure that Laura was more important to him than any woman had been before. Knowing this, he was still reluctant to admit it to himself, to admit that he might be in love with her.

Zero Smith's arrival in Pinedale was the beginning of a new era for him. Meeting Laura and buying the ranch had helped him on his road to becoming human again. Building something, instead of destroying, suited his temperament. He was fond of the new Zero Smith but he also knew it was a little soon to go back to his original name, and much too soon to even consider going east to head up the family businesses. He wasn't sure now if he would ever go east, except to

## Zero Smith

visit.

He liked this country and subconsciously he was beginning to think in terms of what Laura might want. What were her plans for the future? Where did she want to live? Well, for now he would put Laura out of his mind until this thing with the Walters died out, or until the Walters just died. He didn't put much hope in the idea that they couldn't find him, or that they might get tired of waiting around and just go away.

Zero Smith was a long way from the ranch headquarters. He could hunt without the noise of a rifle bringing up his cowhands. He wanted privacy. He wanted to be able to roam the surrounding country when the Walters' clan showed up. He knew they would get the word that he had left the country and he hoped they would leave the valley alone, but he wouldn't bet on it.

Not the Walters. From what he had heard of them, when one of their own was killed they were hell on vengeance. Neither Smith nor the Walters' clan were aware of it at this time but the Walters' vengeance switch was to be pulled more often and harder than they would care to think about.

Well, he would just wait and see, and in the meantime he would read. In his pack were several books and a hammock. The hammock was a trick he learned during the war. It was cooler than being on the ground and it tended to keep the critters from crawling in. It required trees or an occasional rock to tie to although one time he'd strung his hammock between two giant cactus when there weren't any trees.

He was looking forward to loafing in the sun with his books. On one hot day he rigged the hammock just over the little creek so he could lower his bare feet into the cool water. Nearby he had dammed the creek and excavated a pond large enough for him to submerge and bathe.

His solitude was like the old days when he drifted and stayed away from people. Game was plentiful. He had one pack horse loaded with the usual food stuffs, coffee and brandy and books. The other pack horse was loaded with more serious stuff. It carried enough explosives to blow up the whole town of Pinedale. Smith was making bombs to be used against the Walters' bunch. If things got sticky, he wanted to be prepared.

When he completed the building of a fair amount of bombs, he began to relax and enjoy lazing around with his books. He liked the solitude, the sound of the wind in the trees, the shady places. He spent long hours beneath the trees, beside the little stream. He listened to its sounds as they danced their way to the valley floor. Zero Smith was at

# Zero Smith

last making room for pleasant things, and they helped to push his anger aside.

Smith watched the sunrises and had his brandy with the sunsets. He was living in high cotton. The only thing missing was some feminine companionship. There was nothing he could do about that for the moment, so he was resigned to being a hermit for awhile. He liked the peace of this high camp and vowed to live this way several times a year when all of the "hoopla" was over.

# CHAPTER TWENTY–FOUR

Smith rode the surrounding country and kept a sharp eye out for trouble around his ranch. He knew Walters had sent men to watch the place. One day soon he would deal with them if this developed into a full scale war. Well, Smith had dealt with armies before. Much bigger and certainly better than this rabble.

He was content to play cat and mouse for a few more days. He wasn't just sitting on his hands during this time. Smith left his high country line cabin at dusk and under the cover of darkness was very busy laying traps for the bad guys. His second pack horse was loaded with explosives, enough to start a small war. Smith placed these in what he called his killing field. He had done something like it during the war, but on a much larger scale. The idea was to place explosives in such a way so they could be set off from a safe distance with accurate rifle fire. Each charge was marked to be easily seen in daytime and in the event the gang came at night,

# Zero Smith

Smith would fire into a spot that would set off the rest of the charges. They were placed on the main road to the ranch a half mile from the front gate. Other charges were placed wherever he thought the Walters' horsemen might ride if they intended to attack his ranch. Zero showed his people where the areas were and he and Cheyenne worked out where they would both shoot from, so as not to be shooting at each other. It was a carefully coordinated plan. Smith rode back to the line cabin with an uneasy feeling. Now they would just have to wait.

After five days of solitary hermit life, who should ride up to the line cabin but Mary Hightower. It was a hot day. She caught him lounging in the stream in his scooped out pool. Smith was nearly asleep, for the shallow stream was quite comfortable. When he heard the distinct sound of a horse moving over the stones he was instantly wide awake. Gun in hand, he waited in the pool to see who his visitor was. The rider didn't see him because the pool was partially hidden by brush and some small aspen trees.

"Hello the camp!"

Smith thought he knew that deep voice, but he wanted to be sure. He waited and she said again, "Hello the camp! Is anyone here?"

"Hello, Mary. I'm over here. You've caught me in the pool. I'll just be a second."

She rode her horse over to him and said, "You look very comfortable. Do you mind if I join you?" she said with a big smile on her lovely face.

Zero, who had started to get out of the pool, looked up to see Mary admiring him. He was ankle deep, gun in hand, wearing his hat, but otherwise stark naked. Smith held out his hands to his sides in a futile, "you caught me" gesture, and smiled.

"What the hell," he said.

For a long moment Mary just sat her horse and stared at Smith. Her eyes devoured him. She thought him to be the most beautiful and the best equipped man that she had ever seen.

Finally, she climbed down and began to undress slowly in front of him.

Mary, who was thirty years of age, was in the peak of womanhood. She was "lush and ripe" all over. The hard work on the farm kept her muscle tone to perfection and she knew it. She looked at Smith, held her arms out to her sides and slowly turned around for him.

"Like it?"

"Yes, mam. You're beautiful," he said as he returned to the pool.

"I was just thinking the same thing about you, Zero."

She had never used his first name be-

# Zero Smith

fore and he liked it. Sitting in the water, Smith watched her walk into the shallow side and then to the deeper part of the pool. It was a kind of seduction because she paused as the water began to swallow her—first to mid-thigh, then more slowly to her lush velvet mound, on up to her beautiful hips and small waist, then faster until the water reached just under her big, ripe breasts. Here she paused again to study Smith's reaction.

"Lady, you really are beautiful."

With that she glided on over to him and put her large, round luscious breasts right in his face. In a few moments she straddled him and they both skyrocketed to that place where the best of lovers go.

Then they did it again, only this time the journey was longer, less frantic, and more satisfying.

Afterward, they lay in the soft grass in silence. They were both wearing smiles of contentment. Smith's was more like a big dumb grin, and he felt thoroughly happy. Finally he said, "Mary, you really are wonderful!"

Mary was very pleased with herself and with him. She had never known a man who was so considerate and so gentle and yet he seemed to know her every wish. But this was a man who had killed many men. She wondered how one human being could be so complex?

"How did you find me, Mary?"

"I didn't, not really. I often ride these hills, but I rarely come up this high. Today I just happened to stumble on the place. I saw the corral and the horses first and I recognized your horse and your brand so I thought you might be around here somewhere.

"However," she said smiling," I didn't expect to be this lucky today." Mary intuitively knew this chance meeting was a gift, a respite from the loneliness and hunger for physical companionship that she had needed for so long. It was a bridge between her past and her future. She couldn't know the future, but she rather liked the present.

"Neither did I," and he kissed her.

Looking at her this close, he could see the water in her eye lashes sparkling like diamonds.

Holding her close, Smith thought to himself that he was truly happy. After awhile, Mary slid over on top of him for more and Zero Smith was sure that he had died and gone to heaven.

He was almost right. He didn't die but he did go to heaven. They both did.

Mary stayed for an early dinner as she had a long ride back, but during the meal she noticed Zero looking at her with a twinkle in his eye.

# Zero Smith

"Why not stay for a few days?"

"Why not indeed," she said, and did.

Several days later, Smith and Mary rode down off the mountain to see how the 0 Ranch was getting along. He wanted to see Mary safely back to her place but on the way thought it better to have her live at his ranch for awhile for her own safety. His people could look out for her and he could concentrate on the Walters' clan. Smith pointed out how the Walters' people might use her to get to him, and as she had no family this far west where she could be safe, she agreed to stay at his ranch for the time being.

# CHAPTER TWENTY–FIVE

Smith sent men and a wagon over to Mary's place to move her things and her few animals. She owned a couple of good saddle horses and a team. She had about two dozen chickens and a pig. Catching these critters was a lively frolic for the 0 Ranch hands, but they finally managed to complete the humiliating experience and all were safely moved to the 0 spread.

Mary Hightower adapted well to the life at the 0 Ranch and she immediately pitched in to help the cook. She brought coffee and water to the men who were branding and generally made herself useful. She even helped to feed the stock in the corrals in addition to her own critters. The men liked seeing her about the place and about a third of them had a crush on the lady. She liked them, too. At mealtime she helped serve, and then, at their suggestion, sat at the head of the table and presided.

The chicken eggs were a welcome treat for the hands but the pig was considered a

189

## Zero Smith

major nuisance, which he was. The pig, whose name was "Ham," knocked down and chewed through and ate something from nearly everybody. It soon became evident that his days were numbered.

The table conversation centered around the Walters' gang and when they would strike the ranch and what famous guns they might bring in to oppose the 0 Ranch people. Did someone besides the Walters' clan want Smith dead?

They would just have to wait and see. In the meantime, Smith was still looking for ranch hands.

One man found him. The man's name was Riley. He had heard that the 0 Brand was hiring and he had just waited along the road for the Karen freight driver to come along and show him the way to the 0 Ranch. Riley didn't know that the hayseed driver he saw coming down the road was actually the owner of the 0 Ranch and the famous Zero Smith, but he was very careful to show empty hands when he waved the driver down. The two men sized up each other as Riley stated his name and his business. He was looking for a riding job.

Smith was looking at a tall, dark, rangy man with lots of bark on him. He was about forty years of age and had a quietly composed, deliberate way and a twinkle in his eye.

Smith noticed the man's outfit was well used but like his guns, well cared for. He was sitting on a big strong buckskin horse. Smith pulled up the team and invited him to sit up on the wagon and share the lunch Laura had prepared. Turkey sandwiches and black coffee. Riley agreed by saying, "That sure beats the jerky and pemmican I've been eating for two days," as he climbed down. Zero noticed the horse stood ground tied.

"Where did you get pemmican?"

"I took it from a dying Indian several days ride from here who was trying to put my lights out. I figured he wouldn't be needing it any more and I don't cotton much to the idea of waste."

Zero Smith was aware that occasionally a few braves were out to count coup, to gain some status with their tribe. Even a raid now and then but mostly nothing serious, at least not lately. Sitting Bull had not yet pulled Custer's chain. That was still a few months off.

Smith liked the man and by the time they finished lunch, he had hired a new hand and both men were smiling.

Smith told Riley how to find the 0 spread and to see Todd when he got there.

"If you push it, you might get there in time for chow."

He did. And Bingo. He met Mary

# Zero Smith

Hightower. Riley looked at her and she looked at him and they were both cats looking at cream. When Riley learned that the pretty lady presided at the table each evening at dinner with the ranch hands, he knew that this was no ordinary ranch. He was beginning to think that he had died and gone to heaven. This was a brand he would be proud to ride for. He vowed to make himself useful. By the next evening he was all cleaned up like the rest of the hands.

Word came down that there was a new man recently seen in town. He looked to be a gunfighter and as far as anyone knew was a loner. Some wondered if he and the Walters' people were connected in some way. If they weren't, it was suspiciously coincidental that the man showed up just at this time. The ranch people were divided in their opinion as to why he was here. Some figured that the man was here for a showdown with the famous Zero Smith and it had nothing to do with the Walters' incident. It was all very confusing, so they would just have to wait and see.

At mealtime there was usually at least one hint about pork for dinner or ham with breakfast. Mary resisted these suggestions as she had become fond of the pig. She bought him to raise and eat but had long since shelved that idea. Ham had become a fixture on her farm. The critter was likewise seemingly fond of Mary. He was never penned and was therefore very clean even for a pig. The little fellow always went along when Mary went for rides or walks around the ranch. He even attempted to keep up when she trotted her horse. If Mary rode on ahead for a ways, she always stopped to wait for Ham to catch up. When he did catch up, he scolded her for riding off without him.

Ham sniffed and rooted to his heart's content on these walks.

He seemed to find edibles everywhere, particularly in the forested areas, and contentedly munched away as he ambled along.

One day Mary was on one of these walks, fairly close to the ranch headquarters, when she was suddenly attacked, lassoed, trussed up tight, and tied to a tree.

Two low-life hired killers for the Walters' gang had sneaked up to spy on the 0 spread and had been lucky enough to get past the outriders. Now that they had Mary captive, they weren't sure what to do with her. It was decided that one of them should ride to tell Abe Walters, their leader, and the other one was to stand guard over their captive. The plan failed.

The man riding to tell Walters was spotted by two of the 0 outriders and was promptly shot out of the saddle.

# Zero Smith

The pig was so upset he ran straight to the 0 Ranch house, where he oinked around in a very agitated manner until someone noticed that Mary was missing. In about two minutes, eight mounted riflemen followed Ham to rescue Mary. The little pig made a beeline to where Mary was held captive. The men rode straight in and shot the Walters' man to doll rags.

Apparently the bad guy had just bent down to examine his horse's hind foot when he noticed several horseman bearing down on him. He never got up from there. He was a dead man before he could draw his iron and he was soon to be buzzard food when the great birds quit circling.

Ham had earned his freedom from the butcher forever. A latch was put on the grain shed door and Mary Hightower had another new horse. To celebrate Mary's return, Juan the cook, made for Ham his very own special chocolate cake as well as a very big chocolate cake for everyone else.

# CHAPTER TWENTY–SIX

Late one hot summer afternoon, Randy and a few of the young Texans were out checking on the stream to be sure the water supply hadn't been tampered with, when they noticed far off smoke spiraling up into the blue sky. They rode toward the fire and discovered that the High- tower ranch buildings were all on fire. They were too late to attempt to save any of the buildings, but they did manage to save some equipment, some feed sacks and some hay bales that were dangerously close to the fire.

Randy reported this to Smith, who happened to be at the ranch, who in turn told Mary Hightower.

Smith assured her it would all be rebuilt when the trouble was over. She wouldn't be out any money because he was writing a check made out to her for the value of the destroyed ranch buildings.

He didn't tell Mary, but in case of his death she would need something in writing to have claim to the check, so he sent a letter to his banker in San Francisco asking that Mary's check be honored.

Smith reasoned the Walters' bunch burned the Hightower place believing it to be Smith's other ranch. The only reason they hadn't burned the main ranch house where the Smith cowhands were housed was because it was too well defended.

When the paperwork was done, Smith saddled up and went hunting. With his people, including Mary, all safely forted-up at his ranch, he sent Cheyenne Williams to look for tracks around the Hightower place and, if possible, to follow them to wherever they might lead. In the meantime he was going to set up camp near his mine field. Cheyenne was to meet him there just before dark, in two day's time.

When they met up, Cheyenne reported that a child could have tracked those clowns. There were four riders. One was a big man on a big horse and another horse had a splinted horseshoe. The splint was across the back part of the foot and was therefore easy to track. It was the left rear foot. The tracks lead to the road in front of the Hightower place and then back toward town. Cheyenne suggested that it would be a simple matter to look for that horse in town, if it was still around, and then watch the horse until the owner showed. He intended to do just that. No one in town could connect him to the 0 Ranch except perhaps the bartender who had seen him sit with Todd and Randy, but he felt certain the bartender would not do anything to help the Walters' people.

Smith approved of the idea and Cheyenne rode to town by the back trails.

Near town Williams turned back to the road, and even in the dimming light managed to find the splinted horseshoe track. He pulled up in front of the Stud Horse Saloon and saw the track once again. There was a sorrel horse standing over it, hip cocked, half asleep and tied to the rail. Cheyenne tied his horse next to the sorrel and eased down to have a look at the left rear foot. Sure enough, it was a splinted shoe. That placed the horse at the ranch, so now all he had to do was find the rider. He also noticed a very big saddle horse but the hoof prints were impossible to read in the dim light. Perhaps tomorrow would be more revealing. He would track the horse in daylight.

Now he intended to take on "supplies."

# Zero Smith

# CHAPTER TWENTY–SEVEN

Even before this assignment, Cheyenne was eager to go to town. Two weeks of celibacy was enough to tell Cheyenne that it was time to ride to town for fun and games. He always called it "supplies."

Most cowhands stoically accepted the austere ranch life of few or no women, but not a hot blood like Cheyenne Williams. He believed in the creature comforts where female flesh was concerned. He would stay in town for a few days.

After tracking the horse he was riding just at the edge of town in his quest for comfort, when he heard the sounds of a struggle and a woman whimpering. It was a kind of quiet crying.

When he investigated, he Injun'd up in moccasin feet as quiet as the night breeze and found a pretty lady being roughly handled by two low-lifes. The young lady was crying. She was being held on the ground while the two low-lifes argued about who would be first. Her blouse was torn nearly off except for one sleeve and her skirt was above her hips. She apparently didn't wear underwear. Cheyenne saw all of this at a glance and then both men died with their pants down for what they were about to do.

Cheyenne cut the throat of one and broke the neck of the other. He picked up the girl as though she was weightless child and carried her out of the brush into the light.

"Calm down, pretty lady, I won't hurt you and they won't hurt anyone ever again."

Cheyenne had released the girl. Standing still, recovering her composure, she suddenly put her arms around Cheyenne and held on tightly with her head against his chest and sobbed. He felt a little like a father reassuring a child who had suddenly awakened from a terrible nightmare. She had, in a way, only worse. It was real.

Cheyenne didn't think she actually comprehended what he had done to the two men because it was all over so fast and so silently.

The lady tried to collect herself, but she was still hanging on to Cheyenne. He realized that she was anything but a child. She was all woman in all of the obvious places. She had long beautiful hair and a very slim waist. Her ample breasts were pushing into his chest in a hungry way that disturbed him to the point where he found himself prying loose from her rather delicious grasp and heady perfume. He put his coat around the girl who didn't seem to notice that she was half naked.

"Who are you and where do want to go, miss. I'll see you home."

She shook her head and tried to hang on to him a little longer.

"I'm Cheyenne Williams and I work for the 0 Ranch west of town. Now dry your tears and tell me who you are."

"My name is Sally Buchanan," she said, getting control over her whimpering. "Thank you for coming to my rescue. I'm a dance hall girl at the Stud Horse Saloon but I am not a whore. Those dreadful creatures didn't seem to understand that. I usually get along great with men because I really like them, but I've never been hit before or forced into anything.

"They were going to show me a surprise just down the street in a store window. They said if I liked it, they would buy it for me tomorrow when the store opened. When we got to the store they tied my hands and gagged me and I guess they knocked me on the head. When I woke up, I was being carried over a man's shoulder like a sack of grain. They carried me for quite a ways, and finally into the bushes where you found me.

"Mister, I'm really grateful. Please don't leave me just yet. I seem to be getting the shakes."

# Zero Smith

And she was.

Cheyenne closed the coat and buttoned it around her and then held her close for a while. In time she was better, and he lifted her to his horse. She sat sideways on the saddle, with him just behind and under her, the effect being that she was practically sitting on his lap. In this cozy and arousing fashion, they rode on to her lodging.

His desire was still at a high point, but finding the girl had changed his mood considerably. He felt very protective of her. Two people were supplying a creature comfort to each other that was new to them both. It was a kind of caring that often precedes affection. It was definitely a new emotion for Cheyenne Williams and he didn't know quite what to make of it.

Sally, well wrapped in Cheyenne's coat and his arms around her, felt very warm and safe with this tall handsome stranger. Later when they finally arrived at her place, she was all kitten and almost ready to purr and giggle, which was her usual state of high spirit.

"I don't want to be alone just yet. Won't you come in for a while?"

"Shy" Williams had set out for more serious "comforts" than were likely to happen with a girl in semi-shock. In fact, he assumed that a man was just about the last thing she wanted just now.

"Just for a while, mam. I'm really here on business."

"There is no business this time of night, Mr. Williams, except perhaps monkey business."

They both laughed.

They entered her small apartment. Cheyenne found it to be cozy and of course what he called very "female."

"May I fix you a drink, Mr. Williams?" she said, with a husky voice.

"Whiskey, if you have it, lady."

"Why don't you call me Sally and I'll call you Cheyenne."

"Yes, mam," he said, feeling the situation becoming more comfortable by the minute. It was beginning to look as though he had found the necessary "supplies" when Sally brought him his whiskey and then boldly sat on his lap. His eyes were smiling at her and he felt like a fox in a hen house. Cheyenne was sure that he saw the same thing in her eyes, only that she was the vixen.

The next night Cheyenne Williams checked his guns, climbed the steps to the saloon, entered, went to the bar and ordered a drink. He took the drink over and sat by the windows intending to watch for the rider on the horse with the splinted shoe.

It was early but the barroom was already

## Zero Smith

full of people, noise, and smoke. Cheyenne listened to some of the noise and then heard two men talking in low voices at the table next to him about how the Smith ranch was going to burn that night. Apparently the riders were already on their way out there, so he finished his drink quickly and eased on out of the bar to his horse.

He took to the road flat out. He hated to lather a horse, but his big sorrel was up to the hard run and he turned off just as he heard the shooting stop. He was careful to signal Smith with a prearranged raven's call before being seen. Smith had everything under control.

# CHAPTER TWENTY–EIGHT

When the Walters' men came riding down the road bent on mischief, they ran straight into a trap and a world of hurt. Smith waited until they couldn't turn back and then he started shooting the previously placed fire bombs. They exploded and caused the horses to buck so the riders had difficulty staying on. The bucking horses also caused the Walters' men to have rather poor aim when one or two of them tried to return Smith's gun fire. Smith took them out like ten pins. Ten men. Ten dead. Some of the bodies were badly torn up by the severe explosions and this was only the small killing field. The West was well rid of their kind. They were all murderers, rapists and horse thieves.

Cheyenne arrived just in time to help clean up the mess. The bodies were loaded on the horses that survived and tied to the saddles so they couldn't fall off. Then the horses were tied together and led to town. They were released just at the edge of town

# Zero Smith

by Smith and Cheyenne, who watched from nearby in the shadows to see the town's reaction. Unknown to Smith at the time, two of the men killed were Walters' family members. One was the youngest of five brothers, age twenty-six and the other was a cousin, about thirty.

When the horses pulled up by their pals in front of the Stud Horse Saloon, the several drunks on the porch blinked their eyes repeatedly and were about to swear off drink. When they realized what they were looking at, they were sure they needed a drink now more than ever.

They all made an about turn and bellied up to the bar for an extra stiff bracer before they could tell the people inside about all of those dead men outside by the front rail.

At first they weren't believed.

"None of these hayseeds around here could take out the Walters' bunch."

One of the dance hall girls went to look and screamed. The bar emptied in seconds. It was a gruesome sight. Some of the men had missing limbs. Others had their guts blown out. The town square smelled of death.

Zero Smith had declared war.

Joe Walters, who was the oldest brother, examined the dead men and said, "Find all of our men here in town that you can. We ride in ten minutes. When we get to the

Smith Ranch we're going to kill everything that moves."

Smith and Cheyenne rode back to the ranch ahead of the Walters' gang. Smith warned Cheyenne of the changes to the mine fields where he expected the Walters' gang to ride through.

"When they get into the mines, the explosions should take care of a lot of them. The rest we'll just have to whittle down by ourselves. I want us both on the same side of the road so we aren't shooting at each other. No telling how many men will be coming out here. Take this extra ammo for your Winchester and pick your spot. Cheyenne, shoot to kill."

He did pick his spot and he did shoot to kill. They both did.

It was too simple. Of the sixteen men that rode out to the Smith place with the Walters' gang in this second charge, eight were killed outright just from the severe explosions and the other eight were killed or wounded by rifle fire. Most were wounded seriously with multiple wounds. The minefield played hell with the Walters' gang. The carnage was like a battlefield. Men and horses were killed and maimed with terrible wounds. The area looked as though it had been cannoned by an entire artillery battery. The plight of some of the horses was tragic, and Smith had to go around and kill the wounded ones to put them out of their misery. One man had his leg blown off. One was blinded by a severe wound to his face. Some had fatal abdominal wounds. Two of the dead were Walters' family members.

The wounded survivors had enough. It didn't pay to tangle with Zero Smith. The two walking wounded were given the grizzly task of cleaning up the mess. A wagon was brought out from the 0 Ranch and those two were forced at gunpoint to load the bodies and pick up the pieces. They were then escorted off the ranch. They promised not to come back anywhere in the Wyoming Territory. If they did, they would be shot on sight.

The Pinedale sheriff was becoming very perturbed. The battleground was out of his jurisdiction, but the bodies kept showing up in his town. All of these burials were bankrupting the sheriff's office.

Zero Smith slid into his hayseed role, tried to look sad and said to the sheriff, "There's been an awful accident sheriff. These men rode smack dab into an area that was loaded with dynamite. I was fixing to blast all of these stumps, you see, and there was some big rock. Why, it was just awful, sheriff. I didn't know who else to tell. Sheriff? Sheriff?"

"I'll just leave the wagon with you,"

added Zero.

Now they were both looking at the ground. As usual, the sheriff walked away, shaking his head, wondering what had happened to his town.

Only the gloomy undertaker was happy. Yet his grim countenance was only slightly less dour than usual. His practiced look of doom depressed all those in his presence. He seemed to see the world with owl eyes. He looked like a man who should be perched on a limb because he had the blank stare of a vulture.

It was difficult to tell if he disapproved of the recent events. Business had been better than ever since Zero Smith came to town, yet for a man who was prospering, the undertaker certainly looked dismal.

Perhaps he thought his look was the proper façade for a man in his profession. The moral questions are frequently pushed aside where profits are concerned.

Only one of the Walters' family was left in town after the attempted raid at the 0 Ranch. It was Abraham Walters. He was the number three Walters' brother and was probably the most dangerous of the lot. He was the only real fast gun in the entire crowd. When he gave orders, he was used to being obeyed. The only reason he survived the massacre was because he was laid up with a whore at the other end of town and didn't hear the ruckus or see the horses walk in with the dead men over their backs.

When Abe heard all the bad news, he didn't believe it. He went to inspect the wagon, believed it, vomited, and retired to his room.

Walters sent word that he wanted a messenger to ride out to the 0 Ranch with a challenge for Zero Smith to meet him in a shoot out on the main street of Pinedale, Saturday noon. There were no volunteer messengers available.

The Walters' clan that had once treed the town of Pinedale was now thought to be on the downhill side of things. So far all of their moves had been bad ones. They had a lot of dead men and nothing to show for it. To further enrage the Walters' crowd, they were very much aware that not one of the 0 Brand men had even been scratched. The men with guns for hire were getting higher priced and there were fewer of them available.

The reputation of Zero Smith was further enhanced by the slaughter of the Walters' clan and their hired killers. The incident was becoming known as the Pinedale War, and the Pinedale War turned Zero Smith into a legend during his own lifetime.

# CHAPTER TWENTY–NINE

Smith figured that it was now time to send a spy to town to get information about Walters' next move. He chose the youngest Texan and stripped him of his cowhand gear, dressed him as schoolboy with knickers and a cap, and sent him to town on the boniest nag on the ranch.

The boy's name was O'Shea, and he was fifteen years old. If he ever had a first name he didn't remember it, and neither did anyone else. Having only one name was some cause for concern when he was younger, but by now he was comfortable with the idea. He had even gone so far as to tell people that his first name was in fact "O" and that his last name was really Shea.

He was a baby-faced kid and at the same time he was one hell of a horseman. He could ride anything  with hair on it.  Back when the Texas boys were putting the herd together, they needed someone to ride the rough string in the remuda. That was how he happened to be with the Texas herd. The

# Zero Smith

rough string meant the most rank horses, the ones that had never been ridden or ridden very little. The green broke horses were supposedly rideable by any of the cowhands but they sometimes needed the rough edges ironed out. This was the wrangler's job. He made the remuda horses safe enough to work cattle. Cowboys on the trail had little time for horse training. The boy volunteered for the job and he was so good, the Texans had kept him on. He was still riding the rough string, only now it was for the 0 Brand.

O'Shea thought spying on what was left of the Walters' bunch was going to be a lark. He hung around town and pitched pennies with a few kids. He washed a merchant's windows and held a horse or two. He tried flirting with a few of the town girls with some degree of luck, for he was a handsome kid. Finally he got a job as a stable boy at the livery stable.

At the stable, he met most of the strangers who wanted care for their horses. He even heard a little talk. More of the Walters' clan were coming to town in a few weeks.

When Smith killed those four gunmen in the Stud Horse Saloon, he had really opened a hornet's nest.

The Walters' clan was receiving the bad news about the demise of their loved ones so often that most of them back in the hill country didn't believe any of it.

Many of the Walters' clan didn't like each other. Consequently there was less commotion than one might have expected. Still, more Walters' men were coming west and Zero Smith should know about it.

O'Shea got the message to Smith, who was much relieved to hear it. He reasoned that his people were safe for a while and that his was going to be the only gun involved.

# Zero Smith

# CHAPTER THIRTY

Abraham Walters was a thoroughly evil man. This guy hadn't been nice since he was two. He vowed Zero Smith would pay with his life for all the trouble he'd caused the family.

It was the usual Walters' reaction. When they were upset about something, they'd kill someone.

It had become a matter of family pride. Finding himself without his backup people, he was desperate. He built a network of low-life spies and somehow he learned that Zero Smith was very fond of Miss Laura Karen. He had paid a stooge to hang around the stage office and try to get a line on where she might have gone. The stage driver knew of the war out at the Smith Ranch. However, he was not from Pinedale and he was unaware of Laura's relationship to the "powder keg" that he was driving through each week. Nor did the driver know that Laura's whereabouts was a secret. One day, when skillfully questioned by a woman, he inadvertently told where Laura had gone and even who she was going to visit.

Laura was abducted from her aunt's home by two Walters' thugs while Aunt Katherine was away shopping. The family pooch wagged her tail at the two men and was rewarded by a swift kick that killed her.

Laura was a scrapper and had kicked and scratched the men until one of them had punched her lights out. Then he rolled her in a carpet, put her over his shoulder, and carried her out of the house. She was placed over a horse and led out of town. Laura was taken to a line cabin far back in the hills.

The men were instructed to treat the lady well, not because of Walters' high regard for women, but because she was leverage and if she were molested in any way she would no longer be useful to him.

# CHAPTER THIRTY–ONE

Once again Abe Walters had the problem of how to deliver a note to Smith telling of Laura's abduction. He sent a man out near the ranch. The messenger rode up to the hillside above the ranch where they could see him and waved a white flag. Then he dropped a large piece of paper and rode quickly away to wait out of rifle range.

It wasn't long before a rider rode out to pick up the message and returned quickly to the protection of the ranch compound. When the Walters' man was sure the note had been received, he returned to town.

Walters planned to have as many men as he could hire bushwhack Smith the minute he set off to rescue Laura. It all seemed simple enough. Wrong. Things had changed. The price was up, the men much more expensive, and now only a few of them would go against the reputation of Zero Smith.

The ranch was being watched by Walters' men, but none of them knew that

# Zero Smith

Smith was not there.

He was already outside of the compound in the surrounding hills, where he could receive messages.

Todd, when he had news from O'Shea, would ride out as if to check the stock, along with four or five men to avoid attack. Their pattern was to ride above and across a particular stream.

The men rode above Smith's line camp, but never near it so as not to give its location away to the Walters' spies. Todd then put the message in a bottle and floated it down stream. Smith made a catch fence trap, like an Indian fish trap, near his line cabin. He periodically checked the trap, and if there was a bottle, he simply retrieved it. In this way Smith found the note and learned of Laura's abduction.

The note put a chill in Smith's spine all the way down to his toes. It was the thing Smith feared most. They had him and they knew it. The note said he was to reply by riding alone to a designated place. He was to come unarmed and Laura would be set free. He had twenty-four hours.

Smith knew that Laura would never be set free. These men were the scum of the west. They would show her no mercy. She might be unharmed for awhile, but she was just too tempting a morsel for men like that.

218

More likely they would rape her repeatedly and then kill her.

The Walters' gang, with their new arrivals, had pretty much treed the town of Pinedale again. The townspeople had refused to back the sheriff and he just gave up and tried to stay out of sight.

Smith knew that if he was caught he could look forward to a slow and agonizing death at the hands of the Walters' gang. Whatever he had to do, it must be done quickly.

Smith was wound so tight he could hardly think straight, so he deliberately went over and sat under a tree and looked out across the prairie and the hills that he loved. They always soothed him, and perhaps now they would talk to him. He was desperate for the right solution.

As he calmed, he realized that he must gain the same leverage over Walters that Walters now had over him. He must take Walters. That wouldn't be easy. He knew that Abe Walters was staying at the hotel in town and that he was surrounded by his hired killers.

# Zero Smith

# CHAPTER THIRTY–TWO

His plan was chancy, but he had no choice. First, he had to take out the two men that were watching the ranch. They must not be allowed to warn Walters. Smith knew that if Walters was warned of his coming, he probably would never get there. If Smith were dead, the men could do what they wanted with Laura and with the town of Pinedale. He knew the Walters' bunch had already intimidated the sheriff, who was a good man but not up to coping with that gang of murderers and thieves, rapists and rustlers.

These boys must be taken quietly. They were watching the ranch from two separate places, so he only had to deal with one man at a time. Zero wished that Cheyenne was with him, as a well thrown knife was the perfect method of silent killing. Neither man must know of the death of the other or he would hightail it to town to warn Walters.

Smith had a knife of his own and he would just have to Injun up close. He'd known where each man was for some time. All he had to do was get close. Very close.

Smith was no stranger to the silent ways of killing. He had done this kind of thing during the war. He tied his horse well back in the trees and waited for full dark. If possible, he wanted to get this over before the moon came up, but didn't expect to be that lucky.

He took off his boots and spurs and put on his moccasins. He blackened his face and hands with dirt. He covered his guns with moss so there would be no reflecting metal surface, and carefully crawled toward his man. There was plenty of cover until he was within a dozen feet of the man. He planed to rush him at the last moment. He found the man seated on a fallen log, carefully hidden from the ranch side but easily seen from Zero's angle. As Smith got closer he was spotted by the man's horse. For a moment Smith thought his element of surprise was all over, but the critter just watched silently as Smith continued to inch up on the man. Finally Smith was close enough to get into a crouch, getting ready to spring. As he did, he rustled some leaves and had to flatten himself immediately.

The man looked around, but didn't get up. His eyes passed on by where Smith lay. A few seconds later the Walters' man died without making a sound. His throat had been cut and Zero Smith set out after his next victim.

The second man was easier. This man thought the approaching horseman was his partner. He knew all of the Smith hands were forted-up inside the compound.

Wrong. All but one.

Zero simply rode up to him in the dark and shot him. These clowns had taken his Laura, and he dropped them without a second thought.

# Zero Smith

# CHAPTER THIRTY–THREE

Zero Smith barely had time to ride to his ranch and get Todd, Randy and Cheyenne and then get to town under cover of darkness.

He proposed to have his men cover the exits to the hotel so Walters couldn't escape. He decided to just walk in, grab Walters and walk out with him, then ride to wherever Laura was being held and rescue her.

The big problem was to get his men into position without being discovered. They had to get to Walters before any shooting started. He must have no warning, no time to escape, nor time to fort-up in the hotel.

Walters and his men made it easy for Smith. They were drinking and celebrating, believing they had Smith all wrapped up. Their plan for the next day was to kill him slowly in front of the whole town. They were even inviting the dance-hall girls. They had said the whole town would be there. The gang would see to it.

The heavy drinking made Walters sleepy

and he went to bed earlier than usual. He was too drunk to undress and slept in his sweaty, stained clothes.

Smith and his men rode in silence. They arrived in town just after two, with the moon full and bright. One could almost read by the light from it. Somewhere far off a coyote howled, and another answered it.

The town was quiet except for one tinny piano in a saloon on main street. The piano player was being goaded to play by the last drunk who was still on his feet.

In a few minutes Smith's men were all in position, without having been discovered.

Cheyenne Williams' amorous affairs conveniently included a hotel maid who tipped him to the room number of the hated Walters. Zero and Cheyenne simply walked up there, where Cheyenne slit the guard's throat and then snapped his neck for good measure. As they went into the room, Walters sensed that something was wrong and started to sit up. Zero laid his big Remington .44 alongside Walters' head and he went limp as a dish rag. The two men dragged and carried the unconscious drunken Walters down the back stairs, soles up, and put him on his horse, just as slick as could be. Had they been seen, they would look like two friends helping a third man, who was very much in his cups, to his horse. They tied Walters to his horse and then rode into the shadows and out of town. Todd and Randy covered their back trail just in case, but no one followed.

Now they waited for Walters to wake up. It was decided that Cheyenne Williams should be the main interrogator and that Todd and Randy would stand by as silent and evil looking backups, knowing full well that Walters was the all purpose redneck racial bigot.

When Walters woke up, he found himself with his hands and feet tied with wet rawhide that was getting tighter by the minute, a pounding headache and a body as naked as the day he was born, but a whole lot uglier. He had one nostril already split by Cheyenne's huge knife, and he could feel the point of the blade about to split the other one.

Abraham Walters was astonished. He had inflicted pain on countless people. Now the cards were turned. He was on the receiving end. It was several moments before he fully realized his predicament. When he found he was naked, real humiliation set in. He felt helpless and afraid. He could taste the blood as it slowly dripped into his mouth from the nostril wound. Upon looking around, he was met by the crazed look of a madman who was holding the biggest knife he'd ever seen. And it was scalpel sharp.

# Zero Smith

Cheyenne, like most western men, revered women and here in front of him was a slimy low-life that had abducted a fine lady. Williams wanted to kill Abe Walters slowly with his big knife, and would have after he received the necessary information about Laura, but it was not yet time. They still needed Walters until Laura was safely in their hands.

Cheyenne Williams glared down at Walters and softly whispered, "Where is Laura?" and then promptly cut the other nostril.

Without giving Walters even time to think, Cheyenne continued to cut, this time making two vertical lines about an inch apart and just skin deep from shoulder to elbow on Walters' right arm.

"Where is Laura?" he whispered again.

Walters' arm felt like it was on fire. He was in semi-shock and slow to answer. Cheyenne Williams placed the tip of the huge knife under the skin from one vertical cut to another and started to peel the skin from the shoulder down toward the elbow. Walters fainted.

When he revived, his arm was on fire, this time with real flames and he fainted again. When he came to again, he was ready to lead his captors anywhere, anywhere on earth or even in the entire cosmos. The entire process had taken a very few minutes.

Cheyenne softly suggested to Walters, "Take us to Laura and her captives?"

Walters answered weakly that the girl was in a line shack a few miles from there. She was being held by two guards, both good men with strict orders not to molest her.

The look Cheyenne gave him implied that Walters would feel his wicked knife and the fires of hell over his entire body when they arrived at the line cabin if the lady had been harmed in any way.

Walters had from that moment several hours to contemplate his future. He was physically crushed just by his own emotions and his own experience. He remembered what he had done to prisoners in similar situations. There was no reason to expect leniency from these captors, just as he had given none. Yes, Abe Walters had wilted like an unwatered flower.

Every time he looked at Cheyenne's terrible knife he nearly fainted. His arm felt as though the hot flames were still being held to his flesh. He dreaded another painful session with Cheyenne. He also was very much aware that the men he had hired were not reliable and might have already molested Laura. He gave a silent prayer that she was still all right. So did Zero Smith.

**Zero Smith**

# CHAPTER THIRTY–FOUR

The next problem was to get to the line shack without being discovered. They did so quietly and quickly. They rode all night and into the next day. Now they had to take out the two gorillas that were guarding Laura. It would be a ticklish task. It must be done before either of the men knew what was happening, and without injuring Laura.

Todd had previously come up with a plan that Smith liked. When they arrived at the place where Laura was being held, Todd would pose as a whiskey peddler and lead a pack mule right down to the line shack, and entice the two guards outside. He was to walk in, hatless and bent like an old man. They put white fire ashes in his hair to help age him and dressed him as near like a peddler as they could manage. He looked to be apparently unarmed even though he was carrying a two shot Derringer .45 hideout gun.

Smith reasoned that they must first be certain there were only the two guards as

Walters had said. Cheyenne was to Injun up on the blind side of the cabin, peek through the window and then signal with the number of fingers how many guards there actually were.

Todd went as close as he could, with protection from the trees, and then "helloed" the camp.

He held up a bottle of whiskey and asked if anyone was interested. When no one shot at him, he stepped out from behind the trees, leading his mule and holding up the whiskey as he walked toward the line cabin.

Meanwhile, Cheyenne managed to sneak up to the shack while Todd was distracting the guards. He signaled with two fingers that there were just the two men.

When the two guards saw that the peddler was an old man and unarmed, they both came out to have a look at the whiskey, but first they took time to tie and gag Laura so she couldn't cry out.

As soon as Laura's guards were clear of the cabin, four guns shot them to doll rags.

Laura was untied, comforted, and led away from the cabin area by Smith. Abe Walters was hanged on the spot. A note was left pinned to his swinging naked body that said, "WALTERS GANG - LEAVE WYOMING."

Cheyenne would have filleted the man,

but he reluctantly went along with Smith's decision to just hang him.

Laura was found to be unharmed, except for a sore jaw, a few scratches, and a dirty face.

Smith held her close for a long time. There were no words necessary at a time like this. Then they all moved away from the line shack and its bad memories.

They set up a new campsite next to a clear stream that was tucked in some pines and opened out onto a beautiful meadow. There Laura bathed and was allowed to rest for a day before starting the long ride to the 0 Ranch.

Back at the ranch, everyone was warmly welcomed and they all experienced a pleasant feeling of safety. Laura held up very well considering her ordeal. The men planned their next move.

Smith had taken the dreadful leverage away from his enemies. Laura was at last safe. He could go on the attack.

# Zero Smith

# CHAPTER THIRTY–FIVE

When Abe Walters didn't return after a few days, his men had every reason to be alarmed. They weren't getting paid. They had a meeting and it was decided that one of them should ride to the telegraph office twenty-two miles away and wire for more money and more help.

In a long telegraph message to the remaining Walters back east, the man used the one argument that he knew would get their attention: ridicule.

The man explained the situation as he saw it. He told the Walters' people just how bad things were and how many Walters had already been killed. He told the Walters' people back in Tennessee to bring the entire clan to get vengeance on Zero Smith, if they didn't want to be the laughing stock of the West. He explained further that the situation was so bad that the news would undoubtedly travel back to their hill country where the Walters' clan would become the laughing stock there, as well.

# Zero Smith

The clan called a meeting. It took nearly ten days to get the word out to all of the available fighting men. The clan was feared and respected and they liked it that way. Now all of a sudden one western gun was knocking them off one by one and humiliating them all. It was agreed that something must be done.

The Walters' clan put together their best remaining fighting men, plus a few friends and scallyawags. They boarded the train in high spirits.

They passed the jug around and agreed as to how this trip was probably only going to take a couple of days. Then they could all get back to their respective territories where they could continue to lean on the locals in their usual nefarious ways. Just now, they were headed for Pinedale. For some it might have been more accurate to say they were headed for a pine box.

Most of these men had no idea where they were going, nor how far. Though these men were known as fighters, most of them had not been more than fifty miles from home in their entire lives. A few had been in the Civil War and those boys had some bark on them.

The telegram said that Smith was a Yankee, and as all of these men were Southern. That was enough in itself to give them reason to exact vengeance.

As the train rattled west, some of them were singing "Dixie." The next day the train was still rattling west and they weren't singing. They were already sick of it. They were sure to a man that they had found the hardest seats on the planet, and they had. They felt each jolt of the poorly laid track. Each clickity-clack of the wheels was like a nail being driven into their brains. The sounds went especially well with a severe hangover, which by now many of them had.

One man was ready to get off and ride a horse the rest of the way, but he didn't have the slightest idea of how far it was to Pinedale, nor even where it was. Another just wanted to get off and rest for a few days and then continue on. Several of the men thought that was a good idea. A few even wanted to return home, but they stayed because of the looks they received from the other men in the clan. They all thought Wyoming much closer than it was.

They were beginning to get on each other's nerves. Many of these people were not fond of one another and hadn't been for years and now they were crammed together like cattle in this hard-riding, smoke-filled rail car.

One of them asked the conductor when they would get to Pinedale, Wyoming. He answered by saying, "Wyoming? Hell fire man. We're still in Missouri!"

This sterling bit of news didn't tell them much of anything because most of them didn't know where Missouri was either. The men were learning one thing though. The West was a whole hell of a lot bigger than any of them had ever imagined. What they didn't know was even though they had been on a railcar for days, they hadn't even come to the West yet.

After many days of grueling travel in smoke-filled cars, the men were becoming lean on the poor food and their horses back in the cattle cars were becoming even leaner and out of shape from being cooped up. The last rest the horses had was back in "St. Joe" when they were off-loaded to change trains. Even then, the horses were allowed only one day to rest, feed and roll in the railroad's corrals.

Days later they all landed in the town that was twenty-two miles from Pinedale. The railroad didn't go any closer. The Walters' bunch were all a little bent from the arduous trip and too much booze. They hardly looked like fighting men, but they were sure enough snarling, mostly at each other. The train landed them late at night and there were not enough rooms to shelter them, so naturally they leaned on the locals

238

to make room. This was done by kicking nice people out of their rooms in the hotel in the middle of the night. The next day they left without paying, further endearing themselves to the locals. They rode into Pinedale, nearly twelve days after leaving Tennessee, and they were very short fused. Even their horses were snarly.

**Zero Smith**

# CHAPTER THIRTY–SIX

While it was known that Pinedale still had the Walters' clan to deal with, there was now a new threat. O'Shea learned that a stranger had arrived, a man reputed to be a hired gun. Very fast. So fast in fact that no one had ever lived to tell about it. It was also reported that he always shot his intended victim right between the eyes. There was much talk about this man who was so confident that he could draw and fire at whatever part of the human anatomy he chose. It was further rumored that he was connected to the Walters' family.

O'Shea soon learned that the mysterious stranger was a notorious gunfighter named Wilcox, but he had no actual connection with the Walters' family. On the contrary, he had come to Pinedale to kill Zero Smith simply to prove to himself and the world that he was the fastest anywhere. His personal dispute with Smith had nothing to do with the Walters' situation.

It was a mere coincidence that a shooter

# Zero Smith

happened to arrive in Pinedale a few days before the shoot-up of the Walters' gang.

Wilcox, a gunman of some reputation, had been tracking the elusive Zero Smith for three years, to challenge him in a gunfight, to prove to himself and the rest of the world that he, Wilcox, was the fastest gun.

He wore two nickel plated forty- fours, with bone grips, in black holsters tied down on both sides. His clothes were all black and he wore a flat crowned, wide brimmed, black hat, string tie, and high, tooled, leather boots with shiny, silver spurs. He even rode a coal black horse with a black saddle on a white saddle blanket. He looked like a man on parade who incidentally dealt in death. He was feared and he liked it. His gun was for hire and his outfit said so. He was never out of work. He was a man who was high on gun skill and low on ethics, but he was not a murderer.

Wilcox saw himself as a breed apart, which he was, but unlike Zero Smith, the man had neither class nor style.

Both men were good with guns, but any similarity between the two men ended there. Wilcox was possessed by a perverse ego. He thrived on attention.

Wilcox was a man with a big ego and a very fast draw. He had been following the elusive Zero Smith for several years. They might even have stood next to each other or been in the same card room or in a livery stable at the same time. Wilcox was always looking for a man like himself. A man that stood out in a crowd of hundreds.

Wilcox looked like what he thought a gunman should look like. He was too showy for most folks in the west, who tended toward drab and homespun, but his guns were too fast for folks to challenge. Those that tried, died.

Wilcox didn't care about Walters' problems. For Wilcox it was a matter of ego and pride. The man favored show. He wanted a shoot-out in front of the entire town of Pinedale, not some grubby war out on the prairies near the Smith ranch.

Wilcox was a patient man. He would wait. He figured sooner or later Smith had to come to town for supplies.

Wilcox didn't want anyone facing Smith before he did. He made it very clear to everyone, including those of the Walters' clan, that he would take a very dim view of anyone else taking out Smith before he had his chance. He went so far as to threaten that he might even side with Smith if Walters' men didn't honor their agreement to call off their goons and let Wilcox deal with Smith.

The Walters were not entirely displeased with idea of getting a first class gun to do

# Zero Smith

their work for them. Although they were not as patient as Wilcox, they were willing to give it a few days to see what would happen, and called off their guns. The men grumbled about the delay because they each wanted the promised bonus for getting Zero Smith.

In contrast to Wilcox, Smith was a fast gun today because of his held-in anger at his father's killer and the horrors of the war that drove him to practice. Hour after hour he practiced with his six guns. After the war, gun practice helped to control his rage. It seemed to him the better he got the less anger he had. Later, gun practice continued to calm him. Gun practice seemed to temporarily dissipate some of his anger. If he shot up the gun hand of a low-life, it made him feel better.

He didn't think of himself as an avenging spirit, but in fact he was. He avoided trouble with people that looked to be solid citizens, but looked for it among the rascals and low-lifes of the west.

And Zero Smith continued to practice, practice, practice. He did until he met Laura. Then his attitude changed, but he still practiced.

Smith and Wilcox. Wilcox and Smith. Each man obsessed but for entirely different reasons.

Wilcox practiced to be noticed. He knew

in his own mind that he was the best and he wanted the whole world to know what he knew. He would face anyone, but it must be in public. So far he had been better than any man. He gun-worked for money, but more important to him was the show. He thrived on the fear of others and the adulation shown him. It wouldn't occur to him to face another gunman if no one was watching, unless he absolutely had to. Wilcox was driven in his own way toward his own destruction. He could not stop. He would keep challenging the fast guns of the world until he was killed.

Although Smith was the very opposite of Wilcox in almost every way, the same fate could happen to him. Early on he knew it and didn't care. He had pride, but he wasn't showy. On the contrary, he liked anonymity. He liked his privacy. He liked being unknown. Passing as an average man was a role that he cherished.

Much of the time he stayed up in the "high lonesome," away from any towns. Or at least he did until he met Laura Karen of the Karen Freight Company of Pinedale, Wyoming. Now Smith's world was different. He would have to take steps.

When Smith decided to stay in one place, he knew it wouldn't be long before other fast guns would find him and want to test their gun skill against his.

# Zero Smith

There was a time when he might have welcomed them, but now, because of Laura, all of that had changed. From here on, he just wanted to be left alone and live quietly with the woman he loved.

Smith hoped this man Wilcox would be his last showdown. For some time now, Smith had been forming a plan.

Wilcox had finally caught up with Zero Smith quite by accident. He discovered that Smith was the one he was searching for when he overheard two men talking in a bar back down the road. They had seen the large cattle herd being moved and inquired who the owners might be. Someone told them it was the 0 Brand outfit, even though all the cattle were not yet branded and that the ranch belonged to the famous Zero Smith, the gunfighter. Gun news always traveled as fast as the guns themselves.

It would soon be quick draw time in Pinedale.

# CHAPTER THIRTY–SEVEN

When O'Shea reported back to Smith with the news that Wilcox, the shootist, simply wanted a showdown between the two of them, Smith was much relieved. He felt that if Wilcox was for real, then none of the ranch hands would have to get involved in a gun war.

Smith told his people to stay close to the ranch and to watch carefully if any more Walters' men showed up. Things seemed rather quiet since the disappearance of Abraham Walters. Perhaps the Walters-Smith feud was over. He went on to say that if the town still had several Walters' people in it, it wouldn't be smart for him to ride in there to face Wilcox and then get blown out of the saddle by the Walters' bunch. Smith needed more information, so he sent O'Shea back to town to investigate.

He thought, rightly so, that between the two of them they might get a clearer picture as to what was going on with the Walters gang.

# Zero Smith

Smith also decided that he should go to town in one of his many disguises and see what he could learn. No one in town would expect him to do that, not even his own people.

He made a coat with a large hump on the inside that would appear to be on his back. He wore a ratty looking wig under an old hat. He put on a little stage makeup that helped age him. Smith effected a bent over posture so he would not have to look anyone in the eye. He adopted a shuffling walk that completed his disguise. He was armed, but his gun was covered by his long coat.

When he arrived in town, he tried to get work at the livery stable and was turned down. As he left, O'Shea said to him, "Sorry, old man" and the boy meant it. He didn't realize that he was speaking to his boss. Smith smiled inwardly and shuffled across the street toward the saloon and the Walters' hang out, like Daniel off to the lion's den.

Smith went to the bar and purposely ordered a glass of cheap wine, took it to a table where he could observe the entire room with ease, and sat down to wait. He wasn't sure just what he was waiting for, but he was sure that when it came he would recognize it, whatever it was.

Smith was sprawled in his chair, slowly tasting the revolting wine. He looked slept in and wrinkled.

When the bartender saw him, he ambled over and asked if he was looking for a job. Smith started to say no when he thought better of it, and said, "Doing what?"

"I need a swamper. You know, mop the floors and run a few errands."

"What you paying?"

When the bartender told him, Smith knew why the job was open, but he decided to take it anyway. It would give him the chance to watch what was going on.

"I'll do it on the condition that it's one day at a time."

"Agreed," said the bartender, who then proceeded to show Smith where the mops and brooms were.

"You can sleep in this room if you want."

Zero knew that while working here at the Stud Horse Saloon he would be subject to derision and ridicule because he was a hunchback. He decided that he would be willing to eat a little humble pie, if he could find out just how many men were still on the Walters' payroll. He put Wilcox in the back of his mind for now. First things first.

The big coat he was wearing easily covered his side gun, so he wore it all the time. That same evening, Smith was just finishing mopping the hall at the back of the saloon when he heard men talking in an ad-

# Zero Smith

joining room. Someone mentioned Smith's name. Working slowly and listening hard, Smith heard one man say, "I've had enough. I'm pulling out."

"What about you, Earl"?

"I ride with Charlie. Where he goes, I go."

"I'll double your pay," said a voice.

"Sorry, Smith is a heller with a gun and I can't spend the money if I'm dead."

Two men scuffed their chairs as they got up to leave and Zero moved quickly away from the door and over to the mop closet as they came out. He watched them through the window as they mounted up and rode north away from town.

Two more down he thought. He was standing where he could see the hall, wringing out a mop, when the two remaining men came out. He didn't know either of them. He did know they were his enemies. He wondered just how many more there were hanging around town.

As they went out, Smith heard one of them say, "If we want good guns, it's liable to get expensive from here on."

The other one looked directly at Smith and said loud enough for Smith to hear, "Jesus, help must be hard to get. Who's the hunchback in the baggy coat?"

Smith thought to himself, "One day you

might just find out." Now he figured he knew who the new Walters' boss was. He found out that the man was part of the clan but his name wasn't Walters. His name was McCallum and he was another ranked gun. This guy had spent most of his adult life leaning on nearly helpless people. He was a composite of bad habits and evil behavior, so quite naturally he was welcomed into the clan when he married one of the Walters' belles, who, incidentally, was just a shade scruffier than he was. It was a perfect match.

Smith went to his room and changed costumes. He reappeared on the street at dusk, dressed as a miner. He planned to hang around the bar as a customer and hear the talk, if any. As a "townie" it might seem strange if he were seen wearing a side arm, but as a miner he would still be able to wear a pistol without it seeming unusual.

O'Shea had informed Smith how the town of Pinedale was becoming more rowdy and people were afraid to walk the streets. The sheriff finally threw in the towel. He had been wounded trying to stand up to the Walters' guns. With the Sheriff's gun arm in a sling, the town was practically defenseless. The town council was not able to hire another sheriff even though they doubled the salary. The situation was serious.

## Zero Smith

A small girl was nearly killed when she was run over by a team pulling a wagon, frightened by a drunken Walters' man shooting at the hotel porch railing. Decent women were being raped for the first time in memory. Some of the town's leading citizens were being ridiculed by the fast guns brought in by Walters.

# CHAPTER THIRTY–EIGHT

In the morning he awoke with the feeling that he might need to be "gun sharp" within the next few days. Zero Smith, disguised again as a hunchback, rode out of town on a rented horse with several boxes of .44 ammunition. A few miles out he found a secluded place. He then rode a wide circle to be sure he was alone. He loaded both guns and all of his extra cylinders with the deadly .44 bullets. He picked out very difficult targets and began firing away.

The first shots were from horseback and the next group were from the ground, some from standing positions and still more from a running crouch. Some of those shots were fired while rolling over and over on the ground. Each time he hit the target.

Zero Smith worked from experience and he was very thorough. When the ammo was gone, he quit. He was hot and dirty but he was ready.

Like any savvy Westerner, Smith had saved enough ammo to fill both pistols so he would not be defenseless on the ride back to town.

That same night Smith was able to help a young girl. He heard a scuffling noise across the street in the shadows. Then he heard a scream. When he quietly and suddenly appeared on the scene, he found two men mauling a young lady. One of them was trying to kiss her and she was struggling to pull away when Smith laid a gun barrel heavily on the man's head. He fell face down in the dirt as though he had been poleaxed.

The other one was kicked in the groin, and as he bent over, he was kneed in the face. His nose burst like a ripe tomato. Zero then bound and gagged both of them. The one with the smashed nose was gagged so that he could still breathe through his mouth.

Zero could see that the young lady's dress was torn, showing part of her breasts. She was shaken, but otherwise unhurt. She accepted his presence very naturally.

"Where is your home, young lady?" Smith asked.

She pointed and he proceeded to escort her the short distance.

They had to step over the fallen men to continue on the boardwalk.

Smith said, "They can't hurt you now, miss."

With his help, the girl managed to step

over the unpleasant obstacles.

When they arrived at her door, she whispered, "Thank you. Thank you. I've never been so scared."

Smith asked if her parents were home and the girl nodded and went inside.

After the incident with the girl, Zero spent the better part of the evening on the street in front of the saloon but learned nothing new. There were few people out this late. Most were afraid. Their town had changed. The night was quiet. The night wind pushed the clouds across the moon. Main Street was alternately in moonlight and dark shadow. The shadow had served him well.

Zero Smith went back to his room to get ready for his job as the swamper in the Stud Horse Saloon. He noted the wig was getting ratty and made a mental note to get a better one.

**Zero Smith**

# CHAPTER THIRTY–NINE

Zero Smith was ready to go to war, but first he wanted a powwow, to make medicine with Cheyenne Williams. He was going to put the fear of God into the Walters' gang. The gang had treed Pinedale. They had been operating with total impunity. No law and no courts. No one to spank their hands. Well, that was over now.

He sent O'Shea for Williams. Smith was sure he and Cheyenne would be enough manpower for what he had in mind. Cheyenne was to come in after dark and meet Zero out back of the saloon the next night.

Zero's plan amounted to a two man vigilante committee. They would meter out justice for any offense that came to their attention. Smith and O'Shea would try to find who had broken the law by day and he and Cheyenne would lean hard on the scoundrels by night, hopefully without being recognized.

Meanwhile, he started with the two men he had laid out the night before. He hoped they were still tied and gagged. He went back to find the street still deserted and both of them still tied, though one of them had nearly worked himself loose before passing out again from near exhaustion. He had taken their guns, knives and boots the night before. He shook them awake and then cut their ropes. Smith stood in the shadows and whispered, "Leave town. Don't get out of line in this town ever again. If you do, you'll die."

Then he slipped away into the night. He made a mental note to have O'Shea locate and watch the two men's horses. He would like to know their movements. They would be recognizable by the broken nose, the careful walk, and the split head.

The next afternoon, the two men showed up at the stable and O'Shea, always a little feisty, said, "You gents look as if you dived off a mountain into a pile of rocks."

The men didn't appreciate the description. They started to say unkind things to O'Shea, but uncomfortable as they were, they still were sharp enough to notice he was wearing a gun and they weren't.

The man who had been kicked was dreading getting on his horse, but they were determined to leave the Pinedale valley for good. The sooner the better for all concerned.

O'Shea thought to himself, "That's two more down."

At this rate, the Walters' bunch was going to run out of men. For good measure, O'Shea had cut the saddle cinch nearly through for each of these scoundrels, and he smiled inwardly as he thought of the man with the sore crotch falling from his horse.

That night O'Shea cut two more cinch straps on Walters' gang horses and both of those riders fell from their horses when they were riding at a fast run. The men were really banged up. These incidents happened separately the next day, and far from town. Each man walked the several agonizing miles back to town, bruised and banged up, because they were riding local stable horses that ran off when the saddles and the riders fell. When the horses showed up at the livery stable, O'Shea was sure they were smiling. He certainly was. O'Shea was developing cinch cutting into a high art. He wondered if he would get the saddles back. If not, he was sure Smith was good for it. After all, it was Smith's idea to hassle the Walters' crowd.

That same night Cheyenne poleaxed a Walters' man with his own pistol as the poor fellow stepped into the shadows to take a leak. The next day that "victim" had a knot on his head so big he couldn't wear his hat and there was blood all over his shirt. He had no idea what had happened to him.

Two nights later Cheyenne was in the

stable currying his horse when he heard two fellows talking about a girl they'd met in the hotel. It was the same girl who showed Cheyenne which room Abe Walters was in the night they abducted him in order to rescue Laura.

Cheyenne was fond of this little lady and he didn't like what he was hearing from the two men.

One of them was bent on teaching her a lesson because she continually refused his charms. She said, "There isn't enough money in Pine- dale for me to go anywhere with you."

The man was a particularly scuzzy type of low-life, so Cheyenne sympathized with the lady's viewpoint and supported her judgment. But then Cheyenne Williams usually championed the ladies even if they were wrong. His logic was simple. He needed women and he did not need men. The West had too many men anyway.

These particular two men were known to be Walters' hired thugs and, according to O'Shea, were suspected of at least one rape within the last week. Cheyenne was also pretty sure that they were part of the crew that burned Mary Hightower's buildings. One of them rode a horse with a shoe print very like one he'd seen after the fire.

Because Smith wanted to lean hard on the Walters' men, and to do it without being seen if possible, Cheyenne reasoned that the subdued light from the stable lantern made it a perfect place to "lean hard." So he did. Very hard.

These boys were back from a ride and had just stripped the leather from their horses when they felt their heads being viciously pulled toward each other. Then they were lifted strangling off the ground. Cheyenne had simply dropped a braided rawhide lariat over their heads and then over a beam above them and pulled them up like turkeys. It was a feat that could be achieved only by a very strong man.

He took their weapons, knocked them cold with a gun barrel and left them hanging. The entire thing was done in seconds. Minutes later, when they were dead, he lowered the two bodies and retrieved his lariat.

Cheyenne left a note that said, "GET OUT OF PINEDALE."

The Walters' crowd was getting spooked. Something was happening to some of their people every day or two. They were no longer riding roughshod over the town. None of them had turned into pussycats, but they were becoming very uneasy. They had deduced that a well planned terrorist attack was being used against them by a large group of men. Some of the tricks were quite minor, like a cut saddle cinch that caused the rider to fall.

There were several of these smaller incidents. One man in the hotel had been set on fire in his sleep and barely escaped with his life. He'd been drinking and done it to himself, but the Walters' gang didn't know that. He'd simply turned over in his sleep and wrapped a dresser scarf around his arm by accident. This pulled a lighted oil lamp down on him, setting his bed on fire. Fortunately for him, he was sleeping nude so the oil didn't soak any underclothes. When the poor man finally realized what was going on, he ran down the hall out into the street and jumped into the horse trough. The move saved his life but the burns were seriously infected by the filth in the water.

Pinedale was becoming unhealthy for the Walters' gang who, even with the new arrivals from Tennessee, still only numbered eight or ten men. Or they did until Cheyenne took out another one. This was the man who made the rude comment about help being hard to get when he saw the hunchback swamper at the saloon.

Cheyenne didn't know about the rude remark to Zero Smith when he was disguised as the hunchback swamper, but he did know when he was insulted.

The whole situation happened this way. Cheyenne rode into town again for "supplies" and was sitting with a pretty girl at the Stud Horse Saloon. A not very nice "sleaze" walked over to the table where Williams and the girl were seated and grabbed her by the wrist. He then proceeded toward the stairs with the idea of taking the girl upstairs for fun and games. The sleaze said to her, "You shouldn't be wasting your time on no half-breed. Come along and try a real man."

Cheyenne waited to see what the girl wanted to do because she seemed to be sort of going along with the "sleaze." Finally she said that she didn't want to go with him and tried to pull away. The man held her tightly and then slapped her. By this time, the entire room was watching, but no one had come to her aid.

There was no need to because Cheyenne put a knife in the man's throat from twenty-five feet away. The man died silently. He took the man's gun belt, retrieved his knife and wiped the blade on the dead man's shirt. Cheyenne carefully eyed the people in the room and said, "Any man that slaps a lady doesn't deserve to live."

The look he gave the men in the bar also suggested pretty strongly that no friend of such a man does either. The men in the bar nodded their approval, and it appeared that every man in the room agreed. Cheyenne walked out of the bar with the girl on his arm. Cheyenne Williams was pleased with her, and she in turn was deliriously happy to think this handsome fellow had come to her rescue and even killed a man over her. She was ready to give her champion anything he wanted for as long as he wanted it. She did too, to the point of exhaustion. Cheyenne had truly found a grateful source of "supplies." They were both pleased.

Smith and Cheyenne had almost made the streets of Pinedale safe again. As many men had ridden away as had been killed. The Walters' crowd numbers were being whittled down, yet they still didn't know who was responsible. They didn't know who to fight. They had decided, in their infinite wisdom, to burn down the whole town. Then some trouble maker in their group said, "If we do that, where are we going to live? Who will cook for us? Where will we drink?"

So they decided to spare the saloon, the hotel and the restaurant.

# CHAPTER FORTY

Smith had just arrived back in town after another practice shooting session. He'd returned the rented horse as the hunchbacked swamper and was on his way to his room when he heard a terrified citizen cry, "They're going to burn the town!"

"What about our homes?" from another frightened citizen.

When Zero heard this, he made up his mind to go to WAR. Smith entered his room, changed out of his disguise and emerged as the fastest and deadliest gun the Walters' crowd had ever seen.

Smith walked into the main room of the Stud Horse Saloon and strode over to three men who were seated at a table in the back. Two of these men were the ones he overheard discussing him and the cost of hired guns getting expensive. He suspected one was the current head of the Walters' clan.

Softly Smith said, "My name is Zero Smith and I understand that you three clowns are looking for me."

# Zero Smith

McCallum said, "Well, now. Look who's here."

All three men slowly stood up. They all drew and then they all died. Only one man was able to get off a shot that went harmlessly into the floor. Each man sat back down again, dead. People in the room swore that Smith fired only one shot.

Yet three men were dead, shot through the heart. Ironically, the third man turned out be the mysterious Wilcox, a man of some reputation with a gun.

Seconds later, a fourth man at the bar drew his weapon, but luckily Dolly happened to see him and shouted to Smith to watch out. At the same time Zero saw the man in the mirror. He ducked and fired. His bullet splattered the man's head. The bad guy's bullet went harmlessly over Smith's head into the mirror. Dolly's warning had distracted the shooter and helped to save Zero Smith's life.

Now all four were dead, and especially Wilcox.

Wilcox had ridden a long way to prove that he was faster than Smith. He thought he was the fastest man in the world. His own ego had placed him on a road to self destruction long ago. Like so many of his breed, he couldn't quit.

Wilcox had been showy and fast. He had

lived this long because he hadn't faced the best. Smith knew of three men that were likely to be faster than Wilcox would ever be, but one never really knew until each of the combatants were put to the test.

Wilcox's presence in Pinedale had nothing to do with the Walters' feud. His destiny had somehow tangled him in with the guns of the Walters' people and it had cost him his life.

Wilcox believed that if he had to die in a gunfight someday, at least it would be an honor to be done in by the best. He was wrong of course, but curiously, he had died with a slight smile on his face. He had been shot through the heart.

Wilcox's last thought was that he and Smith were a breed apart, but he had trouble believing that anyone was faster than he was. He was to have eternity to think about it.

In a split second, Smith had solved all of his problems, removed the last scum from Pinedale. Most of all, furthered the legend of Zero Smith, the fast gun.

It was time to once again change his name and allow the famous Zero Smith to fade away as he had so many times in the past.

In the Pinedale Cemetery, a large stone monument was placed over the grave of one

## Zero Smith

of the many unknowns killed in one of the
recent battles.  The inscription read:

> HERE LIES
> ZERO SMITH
> HE DIED HEROICALLY
> IN THE PINEDALE WAR
> JULY  1874

# EPILOGUE

Zero Smith reclaimed his original family name, which was John Z. Colfax.

Laura eagerly married the new John Z. Colfax and she did undo his shirt buttons. She spent the rest of her life discovering the personal spirit of the legendary Zero Smith. Laura also discovered some spirits of her own—much to their mutual joy—ones that neither of them knew she possessed.

Mr. and Mrs. John Z. Colfax honeymooned in Europe, where they stayed for nearly two years before returning to the 0 Ranch.

Old John was made a minor partner and manager of the Karen Freight Company, with the provision that work must not interfere with his listening to his "cottonwood music".

The 0 Ranch was operated by Colfax through Todd and Randy, with the provision that they could have jobs for life, and a share of the profits.

Cheyenne Williams was to be retained

# Zero Smith

by the 0 Ranch as a trouble shooter whenever needed.

As for the remaining Walters' clan, they had sent several of their best and none returned. Nor were they ever heard from again. Back home the Walters' people decided to have another meeting. It was only then that they realized just how devastated their ranks had become. They wisely decided to give Wyoming a wide berth from then on.

Zero Smith had said, "If the Walters' crowd come here looking for trouble, I will plant them."

And he did.

Apparently the Walters' people had enough aggravation. None were ever seen again in the Wyoming Territory.

The final irony was that Smith never knew who Wilcox was, nor that he was considered a top gun.

Smith had simply done what he had to do in order to make a future for himself and for Laura in the Pinedale valley.

THE END